MVSICA·FICTA·

Anne Kennedy was born in Wellington in 1959. She graduated with a Bachelor of Music in composition from Victoria University of Wellington in 1979. Her experimental novella, *100 Traditional Smiles*, was published by Victoria University Press in 1988 and was shortlisted for the 1989 New Zealand Book Awards. She has written for both film and television and currently works as a freelance script consultant. Anne Kennedy lives in Auckland where she continues to write fiction.

Tromba Spezzata!

Musica Ficta

Anne Kennedy

Auckland University Press

First published 1993
Auckland University Press
University of Auckland
Private Bag 92019
Auckland

© Anne Kennedy 1993
Illustrations © John Reynolds 1993

ISBN 1 86940 086 0

This book is copyright. Apart from fair dealing
for the purposes of private study, research, criticism
or review, as permitted under the Copyright Act, no
part may be reproduced by any process without prior
permission of Auckland University Press.

Typeset by University of Queensland Press
Printed in Australia by The Book Printer, Victoria

Now, to the scandal of men, women are prophesying.
                                        Hildegard of Bingen

Contents

Acknowledgments *xiii*

I *An Article of Winter: Wondering and Knowing* 1

He set out to write about 3
The wintering of angels 3
A roomful of musics 4
A small size 4
Transport, a way 5
In difference 6
A music of streetmaps 6
A streetmap of men in the possession of a woman 6
The Council of How Many Angels Can Dance on the
 Head of a Pin 7
Hildegard, her blessed soffit 9
The bartering of their wares, a history 9
Authentic and Plastic: after the *Oxford Companion* 15
A woman possessed 16
Loved, left, articles: after the *Oxford Companion* 17
A cloister of birds 17
The Cult of the Blessed Virgin Mary 21
A Child's Primer in Same and Different 21
Ornamental hermit 22
A middle child expresses his desires 23
A small allegory, this time of timekeeping 24
It is winter, what 26
Ornaments of Mozart 27
A cloud encounters a soffit 27
The possessions of the Church and the passions of the
 Church 28
Gregory the 29
Plainsong: an inventory 29
The fall of an eyelash 30
A friendly word from the *Oxford Companion* 30
Her peripheral vision: after Li-Tai-Po 30

The Difficulty of the Virgin   31
Of seen things, a woman among them   32
A dream encounters a ceiling   32
His autobiographical novelette begun   33
The Gift of Tears   33
A barometer dropped on its head when a baby   33
Their infatuation knows   34
The Council of the Middle of the Day   34
The wondering of believers   35
not   36

II   *Knowing and Dreaming: The Age of Chivalry to the Black Death*   37

A universe fitted with soffits by God   39
A job he found   39
The meeting of ends   40
The Creation, The Seasons and *The Seven Last Words of Christ*   42
The Council of the Circle of Fifths: after the *Oxford Companion*   42
Alone in her room   47
Looking about childhood   47
Diabolus in musica, or the strain of sin   48
The snapping and snarling of Wolf Fifths   49
A game of notes and crossroads   51
The Ordinary of the Mass and the Proper of the Mass   52
The molecules of their speech   53
The order of scenes in a monastery: one explanation   54
The Passions and Requiems of their salvation   54
A foreboding: after Viscount Grey of Falloden   57
Secular monody, or abandoning the Virgin: after the *Oxford Companion*   57
To wake in the dark   58
The last minstrel, his lay   60
De dream of a woman   60
Te Deum of Mozart   61
Cori spezzati, or divided choirs   62

In the interval between Middle C and E-flat 63
Hildegard learning the language of a dove 65
All in good time 66
Dominions to sleep under 67
They have no thought for a woman 68
An exhibition of warmth 68
The condensation of shadows 68
Their prayers answered 69
After Hildegard: *The Bright Cloud and the Shadow* 69

III *The Sadness and Dancing of a Woman Entertaining Her Lover and the Thoughts in His Head* 71

From then on there were choirs of angels 73
Dividing the String: the first adventure of the jongleurs 73
The Cult figurine 78
A hindrance 78
The Four Seasons, a concerto 80
The lure of the Cult 81
A wintering of monks 81
Profession of Sleeves: the second adventure of the jongleurs 82
The state of Bingen 83
Only joking: after the *Oxford Companion* 84
If you look in one place long enough you will see a woman 85
The Splitting of Hairs: the third adventure of the jongleurs 87
The way a windchime 90
The romance of Beethoven (never married) 90
Unto Black Death 92
A Sudden Happiness 93
Particles of Dust: the fourth adventure of the jongleurs 97
The sameness of fictions 100
Organum 101
Organum 102

The Gift of Tears Rent in Garments: the fifth adventure
   of the jongleurs   *102*
An article of her faith   *108*
Florid Organum: an allegory illustrating the
   allegory   *108*
After Breugel: *The Allegory of Hearing*   *113*

IV   *An Exhibition of the Warmth of a Man and a
   Woman Growing Against a Warm Wall*   *115*

After William of Conches: a forecast   *117*
An audience with the Pope, almost   *117*
Angels clap their hands to keep warm   *117*
Rapid eye movement   *121*
Fate befalling the shape and sound of a plate in
   a room   *123*
Modus operandi or, after Vatican II, a mode of
   transport   *124*
Clouds, clouds, a soffit among them   *125*
A man and a woman entertained by the weather   *128*
The anonymous monk takes the name of his father, and
   of his son, and of the author of the manuscript: after
   A History of Western Music   *128*
Sackbuts, Black Death   *130*
How cold it is!   *134*
Hildegard entertaining the theologians   *134*
The manhole in the street   *136*
An adventure repeats itself, a difference included   *137*
La Messiaen de Notre Dame   *139*
A bull in northern China   *141*
and Japan   *141*
She is passive, oh how   *142*
Massenet chalks a circle round the female lead   *142*
All weathers, except summer   *143*
On the Land and on Queen St   *144*
The Counter Reformation and the Difficulty of the
   Virgin: after *A History of Western Music*   *146*
Addressing the dream   *147*
Not wanting to go through the looking-glass   *148*
The tenor of their ways   *151*

V *Dreaming and Seeing: The Fifth Season and the Art of No Such Thing* 153

A season laid fallow 155
A magic realist hazards a guess 158
A dominion to sleep under 161
The benefactor on the Left Bank 163
And the woman, as soon as 166
The displacement of problems 166
The Selfish Giant, his winter 169
The long-lost Wolfgang returns from an ornament 169
A healthy respect for words 172
The Dissolution of the Monasteries 173
The sudden caught breath of a windchime 173
What is the solution? 174
and of the convents 175
~~Five~~ Four beats in Arthur Rubinstein 176
Word indeed 177
Loved, Left Bank 179
Eureka, the displacement of seas 179
The earthly passion of Beethoven 180
Espalier 181
A familiar breed of contempt 181
The reversal of everything, even a mode 184
A tear-shaped globe to show they have been there 186
Their complete Pope Urban XVII 187
The Council of Magic Carpets and What is Swept under Them 188
Litotes 191
The awoken by a clock dusting its hands 194
Hildegard disregarding the theologians 194
The moment of his greatest reality repeats itself 200
A blind bit of difference 201
A dour troubadour retrieves his *chansonnier* 202
Dragging the river: after the *Oxford Companion* 203
Divinity: after himself 203
I set out to write 205

Acknowledgments

Much of the writing on Hildegard in this novel was informed and inspired by *Sister of Wisdom: St Hildegard's Theology of the Feminine*, by Barbara Newman (University of California Press, 1987). The quoted passage on pages 69-70 is a translation from Hildegard, taken from this book.

I am also indebted to Bruce Hozeski for his translation of Hildegard's *Scivias* (Bear & Co., 1985), and to Matthew Fox for his *Illuminations of Hildegard of Bingen* (Bear & Co., 1985).

The assistance of the New Zealand Literary Fund and the ICI Corporation is gratefully acknowledged.

Thanks are due to Gregory O'Brien, Elizabeth Caffin, Mark Williams and Maggie May Kennedy, for encouragement; to Bridget Ikin, who made the writing of the second draft possible; and to Judy MacDonald at UQP.

I

An Article of Winter: Wondering and Knowing

He set out to write about her but instead he has written of himself, or perhaps it was she who wrote of him.

(The wintering of angels)

The music, a wind
of that order
the way atoms fell.
It is cold
how cold it is!
an immaculate season
its blessed mother
where it came from
from the Cult. Icicles
cycling all over the trees
the musical intervals
between their branches
ornamental trills
filling the gaps in a streetmap of the heavenly bodies
a man and a woman and the
difference between them.
Where movements of symphonies
are particles, dusts borne
by a mode of transport
from Earth to the planet
Heaven, wondering
is the matter among them
entertainments of stars.
How cold they are!

(A roomful of musics)

How tangible their thoughts are! How that is the matter with them. How everything is the matter. There is always a problem.

(A small size)

They are sighing and the walls are being prepared for paint in the room where the young prince has his sackbut lessons. He is eight years old, the age of a boy, an angel, a young tree, a sapling, a large dumpling, the shape of these things.

"There are children your age in Australia who have never seen rain," says his teacher, teaching him sackbut, one in particular, from a child's primer in the art of no such thing.

In the teacher's house there is a problem with leaks, the seeping upwards of notes from sackbuts. A team of tradesmen, joining the man sizing, have arrived to fix soffits — fibreglass, cloud-shaped — to the ceiling so the notes will no longer escape. They will be stopped by soffits, dead in their tracks, sent back where they came from like thunder bouncing off clouds.

As the soffits are nailed in place, the sounds of the hammering are increasingly contained very well in the room. Through all this the prince plays on gallantly — through the hammering and the sighs and the fumes in the shape of a coat of paint. He plays a little *estampie* from *A Book of Airs and Graces of the Middle Ages and of Trees*, very proficiently. The manuscript, edited by an examiner for the Royal Schools of Music, London, tells him to play *con espressione* and he does as he is told, pouring all the emotions of his eight years — which are the strongest emotions he is likely to experience in his entire life — into the dance; the heights of ecstasy, the depths of despair.

"Oh!" he would cry, were he not blowing a standing wave into the sackbut. So many notes! Notes balloon out into the air and head straight for an exit from this world, but before they can get very far, they are stopped by the new clouds they have discovered lining the ceiling. The notes, thus stopped and born of ecstasy and despair, go mad and boom about the room, beating themselves with passion against any surface they can find. Before long the little room is full to the brim with the shapes of the insides of a sackbut gone quite mad.

The teacher can stand it no longer. In thirty years of teaching the sackbut, hearing essential finger exercises, preparing pupils for their Royal Schools and Trinity College examinations, he has never seen such a display as this, apart from one year an eclipse of the sun. So he dismisses the prince (after telling him he played that little *estampie* very musically).

The prince immediately packs up his sackbut into its grass-lined case and runs out into the sound made by the teacher's house. At that time of the afternoon it is practising its tiles, a wind running up and down the sharps and flats of the tilt of a roof.

"What is the time?" calls the prince, and the roof says it is made of minutes. "In that case," says the prince, "what is the matter?"

And a wind is holding all matter together.

The prince runs home through the cold wind with his sackbut, the sound it makes of its own accord, or with the wind blowing through it, which after all is the same thing, he smiles.

(Transport, a way)

At first there were modes and music was composed in a particular mode according to its particular temperament; also the artistic temperament of the composer. And each mode was made of eight notes strung together, an octave at either end, and the intervals between the notes were like the gaps in families between children — irregular, falling according to the stars or the ill-starred — and therefore each mode sounded different from the others. The Dorian Mode was sanguine, the Phrygian was choleric, the Lydian was phlegmatic and the Mixolydian was melancholic. In this way the modes, they were very like moods.

(In difference)

The first time he saw her she was reclining on a couch smoking a long cigarette that never appeared to get any shorter, in fact it got longer. Its length was the reason she smoked. She said later she was not interested in reaching the butt. A basket of kittens was beside her, she said for the sensation of fur against her wrists. She listened with half an ear to the itinerant jongleur who had visited her bedside. Because it was all a bit old hat she yawned when she saw the crumhorns, the rebecs and rebabs, the shawms, the sackbuts, the juggling act, the tumbling and the dancing bears.

(A music of streetmaps)

The most difficult thing of all was, at the age of eight, a boy reader of fairytales, becoming a vagabond prince, leaving the castle, roaming the countryside, singing and playing and leading the life of a simple jongleur. He never looked back at the boy left behind. He cared nothing for *him*. All he wanted was the lives lived in books. The parting of ways; the writing of parts. He wore tassels and bells, his shoes pointed up towards the stars, and his trousers were of the most sumptuous streetmap.

(A streetmap of men in the possession of a woman)

Men were
what happened
to fall between
streets.

(The Council of How Many Angels Can Dance on the Head of a Pin)

A thought she entertained once never went home but had its possessions delivered early next morning by carrier pigeon. The possessions filled the room, haloed by the expectant hovering of birds like disturbed dust. They were everything, these possessions — the lightest, an idea, the heaviest, an angel once fallen from a tombstone.

"Hello," she said, muffled by the early morning. "I like you but I think I'll never be rid of you."

He said, "It is I who will never be rid of you."

"Are you a prince?" she asked then, looking at his rich garments.

"Ah! See, I can hardly disguise my privileged background! But I've become a jongleur."

"A jongleur?"

"A musician — travelling in these wares."

"A bohemian then?"

"And a proletarian," he said proudly. "I play upon musical instruments — a rebec, a rebab, a shawm, but particularly a sackbut. Sometimes I pluck a lyre. I sing romantic songs. I tumble and twist. See?"

And he did so in the bed, to show her.

"Do you love me?"

"Yes," said the fairytale boy.

"Oh my petit jongleur!"

She loved him, she said.

"Who's entertaining who, then? Tell me that."

Their bodies, one lily-white, one darker, were entwined like caramel swirl or the stems of struck plants. In the late morning they got up and sat among his half-unpacked boxes. They drank tea out of fur cups from the first box and they said the first things that entered their heads.

"I like piano concertos," he said.

And also the last.

"Espalier," said she.

"St Vincent de Pawpaw."

And also what happened to come inbetween. For the

entertainment of each other, and of themselves, everything was spoken.

"The fruit of a tree, a musical instrument, an angel."

He reached out and plucked the space between her splayed fingers, hung it in a tree. "Let the wind play this, not me," he said, like Adam giving back to the Garden of Eden, thought the woman.

"How many angels can dance on the head of a pin?" she asked.

"I have many ideas, but in this instance I have no idea," replied the jongleur, rummaging distractedly among his tissue-papered possessions.

He paused, raising his head, and continued, "You know — my inaccessible princess of nothing at all! Oh my collapsible dream! — At first I thought you very beautiful, but I did nothing about it because I liked you more than, well, no such thing, and it is difficult to act in such circumstances. The difficulty of everything! The difficulty, anyway, of most things." And after this little speech he buried his head again bashfully in his belongings.

"And I thought *you* were so beautiful," said the woman, reclining on the bed, smoking an ash cigarette, "you could not exist" — believing as she did that the world is not the way it is but the way it seems, that the imagined is beautiful, or an object seen from the corner of the eye, that beauty is falseness, *musica ficta*, a note struck on a slight angle. "Oh my beloved B-flat!"

But once they did something, then of course it was done. And then it was spoken. And because everything was spoken, from that day forward, there was never a silence, or rarely. They had long discussions about the uses of pawpaw, of which, to their delight, they found there were many.

She said, "Pawpaw Claires."

He said, "Little Sisters of the Pawpaw, Saint Vincent de Pawpaw."

She said, "The pawpaw will always be with us." Et cetera. (And they are.)

However, the things they talked about remained just the

same. It is the things not being discussed that change. The wind, for instance. When the wind is the topic of conversation, that is generally because it is blowing with all its might in one direction. When the wind is changing, in the intervals between winds, no one notices this nothingness and nothing is spoken.

But one afternoon, all of a sudden, because they were so exhausted from all this talk, they found they had both quite imperceptibly entered sleep, and the intervals between speech; and they slept for the purpose of dreaming. And because they had entered by the same door, they were, of course, in the same dream, and the dream, compared to the silliness of pawpaw, etc., contained the realest moments of their lives. One or other of them — the most practical one, whoever that was — decided it would be best for the pair of them to stay there in the dream.

And they did. And one followed in the other's wake or wakefulness.

(Hildegard, her blessed soffit)

Halfway between Heaven and Earth in a convent cell the size of her thoughts, St Hildegard of the Twelfth Century, the tenth child of a family of ten, was given to the Church as a tithe to the glory of God, and as thanksgiving for the other nine brothers and sisters.

Thus walled up at the age of eight, together with Jutta, her tutor, a woman who had once had similar status, Hildegard discovered that if she gazed at her thoughts long enough the ceiling of her cell became covered in the most astonishing pictures. For years she kept secret what was contained there for fear of being branded a heretic. And after all, was it not better to let them wonder than for them to know (the astonishments, that is, of their existence)?

(The bartering of their wares, a history)

Once jongleurs toured the countryside in the company of acrobats and dancing bears, singing and playing and juggling and telling histories to whomever had the leisure to listen — the idle rich reclining on couches, the busy religious reclining, nevertheless, on doctrine — in exchange for bread and wine and a bed for the night. All were rogues and vagabonds, cast out, denied the sacraments of the Church for promulgating the profanity of four beats per measure, take your pleasure.

Then a young rich boy, the age of eight, the size of a sapling, discovered a sackbut. Picking it up and holding it to his lips, he blew into it, releasing the most astonishing spectacle. Notes flew out like a family of starlings spaced according to a Church Mode. Nevertheless the result was secular, as was the fashion outside the cloister.

The boy soon found that playing upon a musical instrument, which once had been considered a lowly occupation and the preserve of the poor, was not such a bad thing; that the hospitality dispensed at the doors of castles (of his own kind, be it noted) and at the monasteries, now seemed very pleasant. And he packed his sackbut and his voice and his dancing legs and his juggling arms, and he set out from the castle to be a jongleur.

He soon found himself in the South of France. Along the road he met a seasoned jongleur, a son of the poor, all bound in the bright rags of nobles' cast-offs. His shoes turned upwards, his rebab bounced with delight at the idea that here was a *rich* jongleur! And he did a little dance and he said, "I know of a troubadour, has a good budget of songs, if that's what you're after — a surly individual, mind."

So at the next town the young prince knocked on the door of the troubadour. When the troubadour appeared, bleary-eyed, his stomach preceding him under his nightshirt, growling "What is it?", the jongleur saw that he indeed was a dour man. But he steeled himself and asked in a clear voice, "Excuse me, sir, but I am a jongleur and I would like to become your apprentice."

Now the troubadour, as it happened, had just sent a lazy young jongleur, who had been in his service, on his way that very morning, hurling him out the door by the scruff of his neck, so he was in need of a jongleur, a travelling

Musica Ficta
A note struck on a slight Angle

Page 8

LXXXV — *Crotalo*

salesman for his love songs and his ballads and his *chansons des toiles*. He stood back and, narrowing his eyes, took a good look at the fellow in front of him. "Hmm, a little on the small side," he muttered. But he checked over the sackbut, the voice, the arms and legs, grunting to himself, and conceded that everything seemed to be in sound working order. "I bet you couldn't commit a *rondeau* to memory," he said suddenly.

"On the contrary, sir, I have a prodigious memory," replied the boy.

"A *prodigious* memory, eh?" he scoffed at such big words coming from the mouth of a little jongleur. "But could you capture an audience — what about that?"

To which the boy replied, widening his eyes, "I have whole audiences seated inside my sleeves."

The dour troubadour could not repress a smile, although he was careful not to let the boy see it. Here was a rich kid, schooled and mannered, and the dour troubadour was intrigued as to why he should want to be a jongleur, used as he was to starvelings, waifs prepared to sing anything for the price of a meal. After a bout of grumbling the dour troubadour went inside and returned with a budget of songs, all contained in a *chansonnier*.

"I'll be expecting good returns from this," said the dour troubadour. "Fifty fifty — a sou for you, a sou for me. Understood?"

The boy inclined his head to show he understood perfectly.

"Well, be off with you then, young jongleur," growled the dour troubadour, and he thrust the *chansonnier* at the boy.

No more words were spoken. The boy, girded, set off, giving his master not a backward glance. The dour troubadour stood in his doorway a long time rubbing his chin thoughtfully and watching the boy disappear.

The jongleur was overjoyed at his new status, and he strode about the countryside, visiting castles and noble houses. He sang and he danced and he played his sackbut, and he told histories and he coaxed a bear to perform — his only regret that he would like to do all these things at the same time. All was contained in the *chansonnier* of the dour troubadour, but upon these works the new jongleur made much embellishment, and the embellishment was of primary concern. Indeed, the jongleur's excursions into the intervals between notes soon became talked about, as the notes themselves faded into the background.

Now the children of noble dwellings saw the extraordinary jongleur, a rich boy made bad, singing and playing to his heart's content, and they were filled with envy. And before long, they too took up instruments and apprenticed themselves to troubadours. From then on jongling became a respectable occupation for the sons, and sometimes the daughters, of the nobility, albeit temporary employment. Their affluence enabled them to be poor in their youth, their idle moments allowed them to become busy jongleurs — only now they are bold enough to call themselves troubadours in Provence, trouvères in the north of France, minnesingers in Germany and across the channel in England they are known as minstrels. But they are still jongleurs, the generic. The children of well-to-do parents, like the members of punk bands, have taken up crumhorns, rebecs and rebabs, viols, voices, lyres and sackbuts in their spare time, of which there is much, and they are singing and playing and dancing and all are very happy.

The ragged jongleur, whom the new jongleur met on the road at the beginning — the one who recommended the dour troubadour — when he ran into the new jongleur in the courtyard of a castle, was astonished at the spectacle and he set off at once to inform the dour troubadour of the state of his *chansonnier*. Reaching the dour troubadour's doorway he wailed, "The audience has become the performer and the jongleurs — the first jongleurs, the children of the poor — watching these princely apparitions, have become an audience listening to the allegories of their own trade!"

The dour troubadour's wife said, "Dear, dear!"

The dour troubadour himself, hearing these tales of the precocious jongleur, also became an audience to his own inventions.

(Authentic and Plastic: after the *Oxford Companion*)

There was once St Ambrose of the Fourth Century and of the Greeks. He was Ambrose the Authentic because he translated from the Greek into the Christian Church, the Authentic Modes — the Dorian, Phrygian, Lydian and Mixolydian — which, if you go to the piano, you can hear by playing white-note scales upwards from D, E, F and G, respectively. These modes did not exist until Ambrose discovered them and then, miraculously, they came into being.

At the end of the Sixth Century, St Gregory, Pope Gregory I, Gregory the Great (who were all the same person like the Trinity, or as the note C is also B-sharp and D-double-flat), began collating and notating the music of the Church. He added to the Authentic Modes of Ambrose a series of four more modes (already in use, it must be said), and these were called the Plagal Modes and their scales began on A, B, C and D — the fifth degrees of the Ambrosian scales.

Now, the fifth degree was an important note in the physics of music; the universe was fond of fifths. The fifth note was called the Dominant, and it was dominant (and the first-and-last note was called the Final, and it was final). The modes of Gregory, and of the fifth degrees of the Ambrosian Modes, were called the Hypodorian, the Hypophrygian, the Hypolydian and the Hypomixolydian.

"Everything hypo, below, secondary," said Gregory. And he put the Authentic Modes and the Plagal Modes together into one collection.

Then Gregory said, "These modes will be known as the Church Modes because I am of the Church and I have put them together."

He was a collector of catholic taste, in the tradition of the Medicis, the Princess Colonna, Andy Warhol; great collectors of beautiful things, but particularly of things previously held in other collections, modest though they might have been.

Later it was seen that this collection of Gregory's was not complete — but this was not until the Sixteenth Century, when a Swiss monk by the name of Henricus Glareanus finished off the modal system by filling its cracks with modes he had first warmed in the palm of his hand. These new modes began on A and C (Finals) and E and G (their Dominants), creating the Aeolian and the Ionian, and the Hypoaeolian and the Hypoionian, respectively. From then on there were as many modes as there were months in the year, or monks at a refectory table, or apostles at supper. Everything is linked, there is nothing that is not linked.

But to this day, the plainsong of the Mass, which is the bread and butter of the Mass, is sung according to the eight Church Modes of Gregory, his great gathering. And his greatness will not be disputed, and his gatherings shall not be dispersed, by auction or otherwise.

(A woman possessed)

He said, gazing into her eyes, "I can see every thought in your head, therefore I am thinking them also."

She was asleep, dreaming. Immediately her eyelids began opening and banging shut like cupboard doors in the house of a poltergeist.

How thoughts are possessions, and the possession of objects is the difference between being here and not being here! That is the great paradox (one of them) — how the unworldly are not of this world and yet everything is the matter. Everything is the matter and therefore the inside of the head is the same as the outside. For instance, if she has a dream, by the time she has dreamt it the jongleur has played it on his sackbut and its notes have escaped among clouds, where they search for an exit from this world. And that is the end of the dream.

Or it would be, were it not for the nature of clouds with regard to sound, also to moisture, also to light, and also to thoughts. How everything is returned from them — or almost everything — from these clouds acting as soffits fitted with the precision of an acoustical architect designing a concert hall. Soundwaves return as sound, steam returns as rain, light returns as light but a little later, and a dream returns as a dream but with its molecules regrouped. Everything is changed.

Gunter Grass wrote, "How sad these changes are!" And they are, but that is the way a forest sprouts, a novelette grows, and a particle of dust is flicked off a piano, grows arms and legs and becomes the pianist; dust to dust.

She said, "I can feel every bone in your body as if it were my own."

They made love, his body in hers, her thoughts in his head, entertained. How few things escape!

(Loved, left, articles: after the *Oxford Companion*)

The escapement hatch, a mechanism on a piano, is the series of deft levers that allows the felt-slippered hammer, once it has caressed the string, to leave without further ado *(adieu)*. In this way a note from the string comes into the world unhindered, and the hammer is free to indulge in its next conquest — an E-flat, a G, a B-double-flat?

(A cloister of birds)

From the age of eight, her world shrunk to the size of a cell, its Sistine ceiling or that of her eyelids, or grown to the enormity of these same proportions, Hildegard became part of the great collection of the Church. She joined the splattering of notes against soffits, neumes flat-ironed against the walls of the monasteries; her life of contemplation, prayer, embroidery, curated by the Pope of the day who was Pope Pascal II (and simultaneously by the antipope, Theodoric) as part of the great collection.

For Hildegard the hard part was not so much finding herself walled up, as not being able to tell anyone what was contained there. In the whole of the Benedictine monastery at St Disibod's there was no one she could turn to. She turned instead to a brand of weakness. When she contemplated her life of contemplation and embroidered upon its embroidery she became, quite naturally, distraught, neurotic, nervous and moody, given to outbursts of rage and to ill-health.

"Hildegard has become quite melancholy," remarked the Abbot one Holy Day as he watched the postulant and her tutor dully traipsing the long cloister on their way to the chapel. Hildegard was sunk deep in her habit. "I do believe she is coming to resemble the Mixolydian Mode!" he joked to his band of monks, who chuckled into their sleeves as loudly as their vow of silence would allow them.

Hildegard continued to think and to pray and to embroider; also to see and to keep silence.

One day a few months later as she, together with Jutta, once again made the rare trip from the cell along the flute-like corridors of the monastery to the chapel, Hildegard, lagging behind, took time to peer through a grille in the foot-thick masonry, and she saw sky. And her visions, also seeing sky, immediately leapt through the bars of the grille, thinking sky would be their salvation, that through sky they could escape this world.

It was dusk. The people of the town outside the monastery who cared to look upwards at the blush of sunset saw instead a great flock of birds, such as no one had ever laid eyes on before. And these birds bounced off clouds, returning from them as skeins of rosary beads, Virgin Marys, hearts and roses, and consorts of angels with lyres tucked in the crooks of their arms. And the townspeople — who had by now assembled in great number in the square to witness the spectacle — cried, "God has indeed visited St Disibod's!"

The apparitions continued to occur on feast days and Holy Days, and the monastery of St Disibod's attracted much attention for so small a community. People thought the phenomenon was due to the Abbot's outrageous piety. No one made the connexion between the anonymous postulant's trips along the corridors of the monastery and the miraculous formations of the escapements of birds.

CXIII. *Altro diverso.* Page 17.

(The Cult of the Blessed Virgin Mary)

In his youth he was once
focus-puller on a short film

Death, and a woman was the focus
of his attention. The film

came out blurred but she
was of the utmost clarity.

(A Child's Primer in Same and Different)

Every Thursday he wore evening dress in an attempt to bring on an eclipse of the sun. On Fridays he recited the mysteries of the rosary before a plaster Virgin, star-lit by the whiteness of his clasped hands. And displaying extremities, artificial night and artificial day, he drew attention to the details of his sleepiness.

The woman observed these. "Ah, a dream!" she said.

She herself was clothed in the garments of sleep; the pages of a novelette, its illuminations, the body of a man and the thoughts in his head. She formed studied yawns. She studied indifference until she knew all its particulars and could put on an extravagant display. In this way she grasped the attention to herself, her face the blown-up detail of a painting; her heart in her mouth, though.

Whereupon he embarked on the study of naivety. He studied naivety until he knew all its wiles. And now he says, "I don't know anything!" He can but wonder. "On the other hand," he tells the woman as they lie face to face on the bed, fully clad in their formal attire, "*you* know everything."

Therefore anything that happens between them — *happens* — she is accountable for, because she knows and he does not. He pretends not to know and that is all that matters.

He continues: "Anything that might be dreamt I have

charge of, because dreams take no notice of knowledge, but are fond of wonder."

She protests, raising her head, "But I know nothing!" She is no Sapientia, Knowledge, who dressed from top to toe in gold leaf!

But it is no good, wondering has been taken, claimed, and there is only knowing left.

She takes a deep breath. "All right," she says, "I know something."

"What is it?" he asks opening his eyes wide.

She opens her mouth but the idea is difficult to put into words; that they are the same; that within the desire of their difference they are exactly the same.

Later, when he asks, "What do you expect, normal behaviour?", she replies, "Perhaps a little, sometimes."

(Ornamental hermit)

In an attempt to discover what lay between one note and another, Wolfgang Amadeus Mozart, pioneer of the frontiers of hearing, sprinkled his music lavishly with embellishment — trills, turns, appoggiaturas, acciaccaturas, gracenotes and notes fallen from grace. Seated at the keyboard, he lay traps for what he might find next morning, encumbered.

His wife Constanze, always in attendance, fed him libretti purchased from a door-to-door salesman. You may think this is a flight of fancy, but it is true. Mozart would immediately set these libretti to the most poignant melody. But he was never happy until he had ornamented between its notes.

Constanze complained that she never saw her husband, that he was always disappearing between a D and an F-sharp. Her complaints, however, fell on deaf ears. She sighed, continued to feed him, clothe him, and attend to the ever-growing company of notes — which included forestalling their attempts to escape through the casement. For this purpose she had in her possession a butterfly net.

(A middle child expresses his desires)

Asked why he took up the sackbut — after all, an instrument of the Middle Ages — when such a young boy, he replies he always wanted to be jongleurs [sic].

In the Middle Ages there is more than one age.

"There are many points of view, but there is only one view," he said.

His greatest desire was to be the middle jongleur of a troupe, and also the first of them and also the third, and also perhaps the intervals between. His middle ear is highly developed. He is the possessor of pluperfect pitch and has no trouble walking in a straight line across a room. But there is only one sackbut and that is not enough for a troupe of musicians, vagabond princes wandered one afternoon from a castle. There is always a problem.

So the jongleur buries the sackbut in the garden to see if it will grow and bear fruit. Instead he can hear the grass grow, a pin drop, a pot come to the boil, a trill, a distant burglar alarm and the singing of angels. He can hear everything; everything he can hear. His sight just clears his vision and his hearing is such that he is convinced he is a descendant of Mozart. He once saw a diagram of Mozart's ear in a musical dictionary, and it was like no other human ear, apart from what he imagined of his own. He is determined to trace Mozart in his family tree — and very probably Gregory the Great and Gabrielli and Bach and Messiaen as well — the kind of tree that hangs from the sky; the lower branches bearing fruit in their autumn, while the branches nearer the root have long since passed into seasons other than those we are blessed with here.

"You played that very musically," his teacher once said before pushing him out the door. That was no surprise, considering his ear, and his middle ear. His balance has the perfect pitch of a ship at sea.

In winter the persimmon trees lose their leaves, but the fruit hangs on the branches like orange lanterns. The prince is hoping for a similar miracle to visit his sackbut, to speak into its ear, a message of progeny delivered by a dove. And so he has buried the sackbut. He imagines a tree with no leaves in winter, but with sackbuts descending. He imagines it always winter, and it is always winter.

(A small allegory, this time of timekeeping)

At first there were three seasons known to the Church, and the Trinity, naturally, was of three, and there were always three beats to a measure because that was what measures were made of, the ménage à trois of their beats.

And the notation of music and the rotation of the seasons was like a great medieval system of farming, apart from the fact that the beat always left lying fallow, year after year, was the fourth beat, and the season left lying fallow was winter; and winter was never touched. And after many years of not being touched, winter was very wintery indeed. The other seasons, and the other beats of the bar (although to be sure there were three of them) became leached.

Then, in the Thirteenth Century, there appeared a class of musician — also raconteurs, jugglers, turners of somersaults — who roamed about the countryside singing and playing, hawking the wares of their noble masters. Their masters were the troubadours or the trouvères — the troubadours in the South of France, trouvères in the north — who were both poets and composers, the possessors of songbooks, *chansonniers* like franchises, and the possessors of ideas. Their vagabond apprentices were creatures of fancy, who nevertheless could turn out a song at a moment's notice, embellished, more than likely, with their own inventions. They could smother their shyness when receiving reward, which might take the form of a shower of jewels. A successful apprentice might become a trouvère, so there was great incentive to secure a hearing. The apprentice would think nothing of appearing as an uninvited guest at a private feast in the house of a noble, together with his voice and his instruments and a handful of objects to toss in the air, and perhaps in the company of a dancing bear.

These itinerants in nerve were of course the jongleurs. "People", according to Petrarch, "of no great wit, but with amazing memory, very industrious and impudent beyond measure", which was three beats per bar. But jongleurs, they put no store by anything religious, not they. The Trinity, the choir of angels, the saints, the Ordinary of the Mass and the Proper of the Mass, it was all the same to them. They were smitten instead with the art of courtly love, the Cult of the Virgin and the Difficulty of the Virgin; also with the bawdiness of the *chanson de geste*. Their primary concern was the pleasure of the ear.

Now one day a young jongleur, just set up with his budget of songs by a dour troubadour from the south, was following the scent of a noble wedding when he discovered among the seasons a mysterious white field. This field, by the look of it, had been lying fallow since the beginnings of Christendom. The young jongleur, wading about in it, felt that it was cold, and he had never felt cold before but he knew immediately, from reading about it, that the field was winter, the fourth season, the fourth beat, and he leapt up and down in delight and tucked it quickly into his master's *chansonnier* (his own, if the truth be known). Then he set off for the wedding.

There were thronging crowds at the castle. Every itinerant in the South of France had come to find patronage at the rare occasion. There were sellers of fine food, fine silks and scents, acrobats and jugglers, and pirouetting bears. The jongleur stood back and let them perform until long after the happy couple had made their getaway and the noble guests had just about had their fill of entertainment. Then he stepped forward and took the floor.

He sang and he danced and he clapped his hands, using the fourth beat he had found in the field. He stamped his feet and he played his instruments, four beats per measure also. And the new beat flew out of the *chansonnier* and sought the ears of the recumbent audience. When the jongleur sat down exhausted, the nobles got to their feet and asked hotly, "What is this beat that resides outside the Holy Trinity?"

The jongleur replied, "It is Common Time," after commoners and the grazing of herds.

And the nobles, who had been about to bestow gifts upon the jongleur, kept their money in their pockets and instead tossed the scraps of the wedding banquet.

"Heathen! Infidel!" they cried.

"His budget of songs is of the devil!"

"Seize the *chansonnier*!"

But they could not.

(And the dour troubadour, at home, shuddered and said to his wife, "Someone just walked over my grave.")

For a measure with four beats was a profane thing, being not three. And thereafter the jongleur was denied the sacraments of the Church and the protection of the law, and many atrocities befell him. But what did he care! He cared not a bit, being an unbeliever in the orthodox sense, being a believer only in the things that had entered his head. And the fourth beat had indeed entered his head through his hearing.

Now Rome, despite her stern measures, no longer had dominion over the number of beats in a bar. Though it was a heresy, it was now possible for there to be four beats per measure — the Father, Son, the Holy Ghost, and Winter; the sign of the cross accommodating the newest incumbent on the right shoulder (and three times four is twelve and there are twelve months in a year, and twelve monks at a refectory table; everything is linked, there is nothing that is not linked).

Slowly, as is the habit with change, other jongleurs embraced the fourth beat, and as it was heard more the inhabitants of the castles, villages and the monasteries, began not just to tolerate Common Time, but to like it.

And jongleurs, from then on winter was their constant delight.

It is winter, what
should he wear?
He has often wondered, she
knows. They go to a

shop where they sell
china, and by some miracle they have Chinese sleeves in his size.

(Ornaments of Mozart)

A man and a woman on a high ledge, fallen there momentarily on the verge of sleep, found themselves gazing into a room filled with notes and the ornamented intervals between. Through the organza haze they could just make out a small man, befrilled copiously at throat and wrist, also the possessor of a profusion of fine hair. This odd little fellow was seated at a piano, dispensing the notes quite artlessly, but filling in the intervals with the greatest care. A woman attended him, passing him clay which he transfigured into china like the princess who spun straw into gold or the prophet who changed bread into his body.

The couple on the ledge gasped with pleasure. "Oh!" they gasped in unison, though they had recently entered the intervals between speech. They considered these ornaments so beautiful they would have given anything to possess them, or taken anything for that matter, to enter the place where gracenotes go, the place occupied by china trills. "If only!" they sighed.

"I wonder how we could get there," said the man.

"I know," said the woman.

"Really?" asked the man absently, but he was already drifting off. He was only interested in wondering.

Just then the woman in the room (presumably the wife of the pianist) appeared at the window clasping a butterfly net. She closed the window, drew briskly the curtains and there was silence, blackness, and the tiredness of sleep.

(A cloud encounters a soffit)

Sometimes he wants to be thought a cloud so he makes nonsensical answers, the answers a cloud might make. For instance, when someone asks him the time he says, "I like piano concertos," because that is what he would like at that time of day.

In the meantime she, containing a small soffit against conception, recites, "Saint Cloud upon which I will build my Church."

(The possessions of the Church and the passions of the Church)

As surely as Rome is not Constantinople, in the Dark Ages one performance of plainsong was very different from the next. Music, whenever it was brought into this world, was a new creation, an improvisation based on certain codes of musical etiquette — the behaviour of the text, to the glory of God; but not the same glory (and very probably not the same God).

Then in the middle of these Dark Ages, a dove came and spoke into the ear of St Gregory — words of divine inspiration, plainsong chants for the even greater glory of God; and he was, after all, Gregory the Great. And he wrote these chants down in the system of musical notation that had miraculously visited him, and he called them Gregorian Chance after a board game, Monopoly, they played about the palace in the evenings, and after himself; the way music has fallen and where it has fallen to, or rather, to whom. With Gregory, Rome had become the centre of the Church, and the Church the centre of everything, and now everything shall include music, the wind, etc.

And so music became a fixed object, a possession of the Church together with its lands and treasures and countertenors, existing on parchment of its nomenclature, as well as existing in the air like the wings of a dove. And the passage of music was plotted upon charts along with the movements of moods and of winds, and ever after, music, moods and winds blew according to these diagrams in the possession of the Church.

Possessions are the difference between being here and not being here. But because of the nature of notes, their playfulness, their natural wanderlust as they look for exits from this world, Rome, under Gregory, was seen to have tamed notes, as it had tamed roads, souls, words, and bridged the gap between Heaven and Earth.

And this was how Gregory achieved his greatness.

(Gregory the)

How Great
Thou Art

is!

(Plainsong: an inventory)

The night wonderings of Plato
The Early Church
The early morning
The Liturgy of the Word
A speaking of the Word
A need to be singing it
The glory of God
The edification of the Faithful
A tenor a reciting tone
A tenor a man
The unaccompaniment of monks
The walling-up of notes
Free rhythm like free radicals
The Dark Ages, lit
The divinity of music
A dove hovering with an urgent message
The gift of hearing
A saint called Gregory
A stave to hang neumes on
The notation of Chance
The unification of the Franks
A wind among voices
A musical dictionary
A high pitch in the morning and a
low one in the evening.

(The fall of an eyelash)

She took a pillow and typed parentheses upon it to contain her dreams.

"What are you doing?" he asked, watching the bulge emerging from the carriage like washing from a wringer, the typewriter keys struggling.

She shrugged, "Stopping a dream escaping, of course, what do you think?"

As a pillow was much like a cloud he slept there also. Where else should he sleep? And he sighed. Within the parentheses, when she brought the pillow back to bed, he found the dream quite ordinary really, like the Ordinary of the Mass which is of the same text every day, although the music may change.

They made love and the parentheses contained also the wonderful tangle of their bodies and their whirled-together skins.

(A friendly word from the *Oxford Companion*)

> A word may be added in removal of what seems to be a rather common misconception. Because of the association of the names of great ecclesiastical figures like Ambrose and Gregory with the modes, and the connexion of the modes with plainsong, it is sometimes assumed that the modes are a church possession. They are often spoken of as "the Church Modes" or "the Ecclesiastical Modes". Now the church helped to classify them and codify the systems of their employment, but held no monopoly in them. The minstrels, troubadours, and the like, used them — and no other scales, for no others were known.

(Her peripheral vision: after Li-Tai-Po)

In a clearing a clear
ring, a pavilion
green and white porcelain
trees, cycles ascending.
A pavilion, him, Oh my beautiful

Chinese scholar
of everything that ever was
written! His silken
sleeves brush
across the page.

(The Difficulty of the Virgin)

She was once continuity person on a short film on the enormity of the dreams of a small boy. The dreams occupied his days, leaving his nights free for sleeping. The woman's job was to make sure the talent and the crew never daydreamed or misplaced for an instant the absolute reality of what they were doing.

As such she was responsible for the casting of eyeline. The actors must speak very particularly to the person they were meant to be addressing, not to an imaginary figure over their shoulder. They must not muff their lines, and their clothes must at all times wear the expressions, pouting and sultry, buttons undone, that they had adopted at the beginning of the shoot. Another of the woman's duties was to look after the film stock. It was her job to make sure it did not run out into the street, screaming at the top of its voice as the director was given to do.

All this made up a large quantity of things to concern herself with. To make things simpler for everyone, she took some tailor's chalk from the wardrobe mistress and drew dotted lines in the air, arched like rainbows, and coming to rest lightly on a man she had met who had come to watch her and was standing just out of shot.

Meanwhile, her attention elsewhere, the child talent's shirt tucked itelf in and untucked itself several times in the course of a scene. His grey socks leapt up and down his calves like a classful of children being given stand up/sit down drill.

Unfortunately, due to a miscalculation which the woman admitted to being the author of but never fully understood (it was more stream of consciousness), there was not enough stock to shoot the last ten seconds and the film was never finished. While viewing the rough cut of the existing twenty-three minutes, fifty seconds, it was discovered that all the actors looked out from the screen balefully at an invisible presence to camera left.

"Is he not beautiful?" asked the woman, but this was little to the point. "There are many points of view but there is only one view," she added doubtfully.

(Of seen things, a woman among them)

What does he want? He sees everything that is not seen.

"When I was eight I suddenly saw everything, all in a rush," he whispers into the woman's ear.

"Everything?"

"Everything there was to be seen in this world."

Or so he thought.

So he started looking elsewhere, outside the world, inside his head. Since the age of eight he has not looked at the world and he has seen things that are not seen. For instance, the snow is such bright colours, every possible colour, and white noise, also, has this arrangement.

(He has always thought it strange that when all notes are sounded together white noise is the result, yet cars of every colour imaginable passing on a motorway do not make a white car.)

Seeing is knowing and not seeing is wondering.

"And wondering is better than knowing," he says "especially where knowledge is concerned."

The woman looks at him ruefully, her expression lost on the close proximity of his ear, into which she has whispered.

A note from a piano, where does it disappear to when it is played, and where does a dream go when it is dreamt, and where does a woman go when she is loved?

(A dream encounters a ceiling)

Left to go unhindered, unguarded, a dream — like sounds without soffits and unrequited love — eventually comes to a place where it passes from this world to the next, and flourishes there in all its radiance.

But given the interference of soffits, lovers, ceilings, visions appear, the dreams of the next world contained in this.

(His autobiographical novelette begun)

I wondered
 knowing
   as
 a cloud

(The Gift of Tears)

And the condensation from her visions collected on the ceiling and ran down the walls of the cell where she was confined. And Hildegard understood this as power through the weakness of the female sex, and she continued to weep, quietly, so as not to attract attention.

But a monk, Volmar, visiting the cell to tutor in Latin, felt a coldness, a dampness, and he saw the miserable wetness of the walls. And touching the stone with the tip of his finger, tasting it, he recognised the salty tang of tears.

Although he kept faith, told no one for fear she should be excommunicated, he said to himself, "Hildegard indeed has the Gift!"

(A barometer dropped on its head when a baby)

He has taken a great leap towards the logic a cloud has ("Oh my dear rained upon!"), although once he adopted the mannerisms of a piece of china, an ornament on a shadow box, this because it was cold. Becoming a prince was another of his affectations, along with reading a book while walking in the street (a book of letters gets him very cheaply from A to B). He has studied eccentricity until the self-denial of it and the self-centredness of it meet in the middle and shake hands. All the while it is very cold.

"What are you thinking about?" asks the woman.

He turns to her and says, "If you wonder you can wonder anything, anything is possible. But if you know — well, you know all things and all things may not amount to very much. Then again, if you only *knew*, there would be everything, everything that matters."

Later she asked him the time and he replied, "I like piano concertos and I would like to know one, just once in my life, off-by-heart, and play it with none of the mistakes of my heart but with all its ornaments."

She said, "Oh my china prince, what if the wind were to change!"

Or if the current Mode, eight notes travelling towards Heaven, were not the one they had boarded for the passage of their love?

Their infatuation knows no bounds, apart from he is a man and she is a woman; as simple as that. With others it is more complicated, but here they need look no further than the difference between them, how their bodies cast into the heavens are drawn like magnets, opposites; their imaginations like magnets, the same, repelled in these delicate fields ("Oh my gold watch stopped in the middle of an afternoon!")

(The Council of the Middle of the Day)

The primary concern
of the Algonquin Round

Table over lunch is
how many playwrights

can meet at the end
of their wits and

still write a play?

(The wondering of believers)

For a princely sum he will tell you everything. How he came to be a prince and how he came to be a china one and how he became a jongleur — also, how eventually he took a fancy to being many of them — all this he will tell you in due course. Or she will. Or she will

(not)

II

Knowing and Dreaming: The Age of Chivalry to the Black Death

(A universe fitted with soffits by God)

Then God deemed that a day would be the length of time it took to dry a lineful of washing; and that rain would return to the Earth; and that sounds would return also, bouncing off clouds. And clouds of many descriptions would contain many descriptions.

A man and a woman containing a dream that described their sleeplessness, found themselves vacated by the dream. The dream left their bodies in search of an exit from this world. Their bodies were left knowing the details of each other, their souls wondering what might return to them.

And the dream, fleeing, encountered the soffits fitted by God to stop escape from this world. These soffits were there so that everything, everything that matters, would linger long enough to witness the miracle of great things reflected, in the form of a vision, a music, the body and soul of another, a lover. The dream, at first finding no exit, persisted in searching for a soft spot in the soffits, through which to make its great escape.

The man and the woman, clasping each other, were pulled along in the dream's wake.

A job he found
became him

it suited
down to the ground

he was buried there
with it.

(The meeting of ends)

Though his chosen profession is that of a jongleur, he finds he cannot make a living at it. "It was not thus in the Middle Ages," he complains. He blames capitalism. Now he travels every day to a factory on the outskirts of town and to pass the time during the journey he reads from miniature musical scores borrowed from a life-sized musical library.

One day when he happens to look up from a well-known cadence of the pluperfect persuasion (If only I had had . . .!) he notices several other passengers in the bus are reading scores also, keeping in time with the tapping of a foot, the trapezing of a finger. The result is a complex rhythm, quite by chance, rather than the predictability of the notated Gregorian plainsong. But the bus company, perceiving an overall plan in the order of this randomness, has thought to fix music stands to the backs of the seats so their patrons can better turn the pages without missing a beat.

The prince nods civilly at Arthur Rubinstein, a nodding acquaintance, who also happens to be looking up from the score he is reading, just across the aisle. Rubinstein is on his way to the job in the light industrial zone which he needs to make ends meet. He once confessed to the prince, in a burst of emotion as they waited together at the bus stop on a cold morning, stamping their feet and clapping their gloved hands in a muffled applause, that his real passion was the piano.

In the factory the prince is engaged in the manufacture of china ballet dancers, shepherds, string quartets of monkeys in red vests, baskets full of roses, living-room furniture complete with pianos, and single china shoes the size a fairy might wear. Sometimes he believes the atomic structure that allows these objects to exist — the china ornaments, the factory, the bus trip, Arthur Rubinstein and the members of the orchestra, the imagined notes — to be a minor miracle — until he happens to glimpse the way people move about stiffly when it is cold in the crisscross patterns cast by the emptiness of their trellis gardens in winter, as if ornaments on a shadow box. Then he remembers he too is fragile, might at any moment shatter into a thousand pieces. "Such is the human condition," he sighs.

When he has finished a batch of ballerinas he dispatches them to the tinting department where they are painted in various shades of ballerina and of ballet dancer. He is very bored. Oh how boring his life is! He is so bored that at morning tea time he tells his workmates, I am in love! As this makes no impact he tells them he is a jongleur in the South of France, but that is no more to the point.

To amuse himself, every time he sees a pink ballerina coming off the production line he sings a Middle C, because middle is what he is and middle is what he likes to be, and also because pink is the most common colour amongst ballerinas and he feels in need of a good tonic. After a while, to make variety, he decides that every time he sees a yellow ballerina he will sing an E-flat, and every time he sees a blue ballet *dancer* (more rarely) he will sing a G-natural, and that is exactly what he does.

Hopping up and down this minor triad, a triumph over boredom, a little game he uses to relieve the tedium, also to relive it, the prince attempts to make sense of this world. To the same end he is writing a novelette in his spare time. His primary concern is point of view (angels dancing upon it), and point of view is something he is an expert on. He is acquainted with many of them, knows them and dreams them and can hold forth on a number of them at any one time (the pity of it is, there is only one time). Getting carried away, he leaps onto the conveyor belt, strikes a pose, and is carried glaring around the factory like the many replicas of Dresden figurines.

"There are many points of view but there is only one view," he says to the passing workers. ("There are many points of view etc.," chime his likenesses, following in his wake.)

No one notices. (He once threw a plate at a woman. It missed and slid down a wall.)

There are many of him. He has always known this.

The way ends meet: once, at the age of eight, he became a vagabond prince after reading fairytales. Then he began jongling. Now, in his present employment, it is a small matter to become replicated; fey, breakable, an ornament. This affectation, as it turns out, comes in very useful.

(*The Creation, The Seasons* and *The Seven Last Words of Christ*)

He believes he has created himself in his own image. This is how he became they. An article of winter is something they put on when the weather gets colder. Why is it cold? Because they are china. Why are they china? Because a train passes any given point and the air is the colour of sand — a sand, that is, with glints in it like points of air.

"Oh my fairytale boy!" cried the woman. "Where are you?"

He was right beside her, but he was no longer in one place. He was they. They, watching her, could not bring themselves to answer but shed seventeen tears, which is not very many for seventeen china princes, they said afterwards.

"Oh my china prince!" wailed the woman.

They have on every article of clothing they can find. It is cold. The sea is very bright. Also the motorway is very noisy *but it is not a white car.*

"Oh my petit jongleur!" called the woman.

("Oh my collapsible dream!" whispered one of the china princes to the disapproval of the others.) (A dim view.)

(The Council of the Circle of Fifths: after the *Oxford Companion*)

It was Pythagorus who discovered the imperfection perfection makes, this with regard to the nature of sound, and thus set in motion the slow quest for perfection by blinding hearing.

If a stretched string plucked makes a note, the string divided in half makes the note an interval of a fifth above

He Studied Naivety until he knew all its wites

page 21

XXXV

Tubo Cochleato

the original note. The string divided in half again makes the interval of a fifth above the fifth. By the time this division is done many times, six times, the notes can be shuffled together to form one scale with the original note, only an octave higher, at the top.

Or it *should* be the original note. Oh the difficulty of everything! There is always a problem. The last note is actually a fraction higher than the first; it is "stretched", straining towards a limit in an attempt to take as much from the laws of physics as they will give. The two notes, an octave apart but going under the same name as if married, seem out of tune with each other. And they are. At least, that is the way our ears receive them, grasping hold of the improper entanglements between two unsynchronised sound waves.

This is the way hearing is seen; the way it is; how the circle of fifths, of nature, is at odds with itself.

The Council of the Circle of Fifths was a round table on the physics of music, and what was to be done about it, just as the Council of How Many Angels Can Dance on the Head of a Pin was to discuss what was to be done about wondering and knowing. And what *was* to be done? They could not go on with this out-of-tuneness, the sparring of one note with its partner; the breakdown of the family. The interval of the Perfect Fifth was ironically a recipe for disaster.

For several centuries this matter was pondered. There is no hurrying the formation of doctrine. Early on it was suspected the solution lay in the creation of molecules. If one atom could fit around another in a glass phial, compromising, laying aside a little of itself, then through this alchemy there would perhaps be harmony. But how to find the equation! Entire lives went by — the careers of travelling musicians, itinerants in perfection, the composers and counter-tenors attached to the abbeys of the Church — lives in which there was no consonance (but nevertheless, perhaps, the ultimate perfection).

At the same time there was social upheaval — this in the sunset just before Bach — the freeing of the serfs, the

Dissolution of the Monasteries, the Black Death, the Great Fire, the Great Schism.

By the time of Bach, by 1720, when the Middle Ages were gathering about them something to be in the middle of, the scale had been tampered with; set on its side, prodded, poked, held upside down and shaken until everything fell out of its pockets — a collection of silver sharps and flats. And it had been tempered; that is, set a little flat, each interval contracted, the opposite of stretching, to compensate for the stretching dealt it by nature.

So strenuously had the scale been scaled, that when Bach produced his *Well-tempered Klavier*, a celebration of the urging into existence of twenty-four different keys, all sounding much the same — also the celebration of his life, this in the middle of his life — the octaves were all in tune with each other, and the intervals between all the notes were the same.

This sameness was the semitone, and between every note on the keyboard of Bach was this semitone. And between every key or collection of notes, where there had once been difference, there was sameness.

Now there was instated the little democracy of the tempered scale. Now a scale could start on any note and sound the same as its neighbour, whereas the old modes had had (*If only!*) personalities of their own, perhaps at odds with the others — an imperfection and, inevitably, a pluperfection. To facilitate this tempering there was required a tinkering in the matter of sharps and flats (the raising or lowering of a note) and these sharps and flats, once known as *musica ficta*, were now called accidentals.

But they were not accidents at all. This perfection was very deliberate, an allegory of hearing; the way hearing is retold to make of imperfection, perfection, to make of difference, sameness.

And from then on the hearing of difference between one key and another required a special sort of hearing, a stretching of the imagination akin to the original, natural stretching or fifths.

(Alone in her room)

St Hildegard of the Twelfth Century and of the walling up of nuns and of her visions left undescribed on the ceiling of her cell — when she entered the convent (this at the age of eight), unbeknown to her, became party to an image of herself defined by a group of men who knew nothing of women, apart from what they thought they might like.

And what would they like? They put their hands to their temples to consider. Perhaps a softness and a roundness remembered from their own mothers; however not a woman given to outbursts of emotion; meek in all things, of sanguine temperament; of no great wit, but the possessor of an astonishing beauty, alabaster, easily replicated; also of a chastity to compare with their own; available to all, the risque subject of the art of courtly love, in four beats per measure, in which all men, especially celibate ones, could take their pleasure.

But Hildegard of the avant garde at the age of eight, knowing nothing of the musings of these men and the power of the Church to put musings among its possessions, set about the manufacture of her own imagery and this she projected onto a ceiling lined with the soffits of her confinement; and there she beheld the greatest enlightenment. At the same time she discovered that her eyes were opened to the blackest of darknesses. It could not be one way without the other. If you see you will see everything.

What Hildegard saw on her ceiling she will tell you all in good time.

(Looking about childhood)

A child of eight
the eyes of a fly

the length of a
cigarette
          increasingly

of its ash
> he discovered
a plate in a room

makes the sound of a
plate in a room.

(*Diabolus in musica,* or the strain of sin)

In the beginning there were modes — eight notes in a row, moody — and these modes were collected by Ambrose, later by Gregory the Great, to be used in the service of the Church in all their apparent simplicity. But before long it appeared that all was not so simple. There is always a problem. Oh the difficulty of everything!

The modes — which might have at first been considered perfect because, like all things, they had come from God, for the glory of God — had in fact been corrupted by the influence of the Devil entering the Garden of Eden. When he heard the beautiful strains of an Aeolian windchime in all its perfection, Satan was jealous of God's infinite goodness, and he reared up in rage and cast imperfection into the physical nature of sound. And from then on, sound was stained with the stain of original instruments.

The problem was three-fold, or at least this was the way it was seen by the Church, for which there was always this Trinity, this ménage à trois, even where the Devil was concerned.

One: The most fundamental flaw was that of the interval of the diminished fifth, occurring between B and F. This particular pairing, when sounded together, was unpleasant, jarring to the ear, a ship wrecked on sound waves. A diminished fifth played to a roomful of children will send them into hyperactive mode; played to a gathering of the aged, will hasten them to their deaths. This mortal interval (or Tritone, after its trinity of tones) became known as the Wolf Fifth, or *diabolus in musica*, denoting the Devil. And the Devil roamed about the blessed manuscripts of monks and those of devout musicians, seeking whom he may devour.

Two: Another manifestation of the imperfection of sound was the unstable B. It never sounded quite right, in no matter what company, and the other notes tiptoed gingerly around it, fearing the slightest upset or jest might send it hysterical.

Three: Another, which presented itself much later, was the sad/happy clash. When a piece of music ended on a minor chord (minor as in sad, rather than inconsequential) there was trouble because the harmonic make-up of the tonic or Final note included (as with all notes) a *major* third. The resultant clash of major and minor thirds was almost imperceptible even to the musician, but to the keen ears of music theorists it was glaringly obvious.

Something must be done with these imperfections. The make-up of the universe, its shadows, blushes, beauty spots and seams of lead, were threatened with catastrophe.

To begin with, the unstable B was given shock treatment to change its nature, make it a little more subdued, more malleable in the presence of its peers. It appeared next morning in its dressing gown, toned down; a B-flat.

The occurrence of the Wolf Fifth was likewise tempered by the lowering of B by a semitone.

And the clashing cadence was later absolved by a contrivance called the *Tierce de Picardie*, or "A Sudden Happiness" (q.v.).

These small adjustments, sacrifices to compensate for the influence of the Devil, were called *musica ficta*, false music, because they were not the way music had been created. The old proverb goes:

Mi contra fa
Diabolus in Musica

And thus perfection was made of imperfection and the Church sat back satisfied it had conquered the Devil.

(The snapping and snarling of Wolf Fifths)

A sister of the order of the Sacred Heart, Wellington, New Zealand, was once frightened by a wolf as she dressed in her cell. She glimpsed him behind her, caught in a mirror that hung on the wall. Her first thought was of a wild dog, escaped either from the forest of radiata pine that grew beside the convent, or from the forests of Europe along with her faith. She turned and saw that he leaned towards her, his coat bedraggled, his chops salivating. Then she remembered there was no mirror on the wall as the order forbade the trappings of vanity.

Now this sister was a devout woman who had once entertained the Virgin Mary in her cell. It was not the weak but the unworldly whom the Devil sought to devour as he roamed the world in wolf's clothing. He tested his strength, evil over good, strife over peace, dissonance over consonance. And there was a great stirring in the air, emanating from the wolf, and the nun was struck with terror and put her hands to her ears to protect herself from the demonic barking. And she prayed to God that the barking would not enter her spirit through her most vulnerable part, her hearing, and take possession of her. She prayed with all her might, and her prayer called upon the power of the Circle of Fifths to surround her, with its repertoire of plainsong and motets, sacred and profane, to ward off the Devil. And there was a great struggle and fury in the air between sound and spirit, between barking and singing. But because God had created the world He was the stronger, and the Devil, being the imposter, was weaker, and the sister knew that good would eventually win over evil in the battle of the skies.

And sure enough, before long the beast began writhing in agony and the nun took her hands cautiously from her ears to discover the air was now filled with the strains of a choir of angels, singing in the tonality of God — the same tonality Pythagorus once took a leap of faith towards, landing on it in all knowledge that it remained a mystery. And now angels sang with their scales tempered, and they employed *musica ficta* to avoid Wolf Fifths. And the Devil in wolf's clothing could not endure the sound and, yowling and braying, he beat a hasty retreat, leaving the sister of the Sacred Heart to resume her dressing. This she did demurely in the absence of her reflection.

(A game of notes and crossroads)

It is the rush hour but the traffic is travelling especially slowly. A motorway flows past the bedroom which the china princes share with the woman; five lanes either side of a grass verge. China princes, being jongleurs in their chosen profession, invent a musical game to pass the time. They could talk to the woman but, well, she is so stifling. Love is suffocating! is their opinion. ("Oh my everlasting princess of nothing at all!" wails a soft jongleur. The others shush him.)

A more practical jongleur runs through the rules of the game, in the interests of clarity. There are, after all, many points of view. He stands on a box.

"When a pink car passes, one person plays a Middle C on his sackbut. Got it?"

"Got it," chant the other jongleurs.

"When a yellow car passes someone else plays an E-flat on his sackbut. Okay?"

"Okay."

"When a blue car passes a third person plays a G-flat, and when a green car passes a fourth plays a B-double-flat."

Jongleurs are very pleased with their recently acquired sackbuts, the fruit of a tree. They begin to play. There are many sackbuts, many cars, many colours, therefore, many notes. The result is a jazz-sounding arpeggio, quite by chance: "chance music". But when a white car passes all the jongleurs play together (*tutti*), making a terrible racket. They wonder why every note sounded at once makes white noise, yet a stream of cars passing randomly, of many colours, does not make a white car.

"Another paradox is, it is the rush hour and the traffic is travelling particularly slowly," remarks a thoughtful jongleur wearing spectacles.

They once loved a woman, but who she was had nothing to do with it, her person. She could have been anyone and they would have imagined her this way. In the *Ficta* you will only ever hear her referred to as the woman; there is no hope of ever getting to know her.

"It is no use building up expectations," adds the china prince who was on the verge of tears when they first became many. "Only to be dashed."

(The Ordinary of the Mass and the Proper of the Mass)

In the Proper of the Mass (the parts of the Mass that do not change) were the *Introit*, the *Gradual*, the *Alleluia*, the *Tract*, the *Offertory*, the *Communion* and the *Ite missa est*.

The Ordinary of the Mass, which changed according to the season, contained the *Kyrie*, the *Gloria*, the *Credo*, the *Sanctus*, the *Benedictus* and the *Agnus Dei*.

It was all very proper and it was all, of course, very ordinary as well.

But how they loathe this life! How ordinary it all is and how inappropriate, considering there is a map of the universe they drew once and their lives are not going according to it. (The inside of the head is the same as the outside.) They should be jongling, but here they are working in a china factory. Then there is the woman whom they expend so much love on and who, according to the grand plan, should resemble the Virgin Mary in all things apart from the way she uses her body — well, they may as well love themselves for all the good she does them.

"Selfish!" explodes one of the china princes, and the others nod enthusiastically in agreement.

"And insensitive."

"Despite everything."

"Yes, everything!"

As a diversion they read musical scores on the way to and from the factory, and play musical games at home. Also they are writing a novelette which they have been writing for a number of years. The number of years is eight, soon to change to nine. The most changeable thing about the novelette is its length, in years, which is not so much a growth as a progression into the finite like the increase of ash on the end of a burning cigarette. But china princes are very proud of these years, and the small affectation of the angle at which they are held, and every year they throw a party to celebrate the number of them the novelette has been in the writing.

What is the novelette about? ask the guests (understandably).

It is about, well, china princes will tell you all in good time. What is important about the novelette is that it is unfinished. It is more use that way, and more amusing. When it is complete it will no longer be a diversion from the tedium of this life.

"Well, perhaps we could just say one thing about it," begins one of the china princes, "and that is, it contains songs, poems and histories, also dances and the pirouettes of bears, much like the contents of a *chansonnier*, in fact. And it is called *Musica Ficta* after a certain falseness in music, and indeed in all things."

"And another thing," says another, "its subject is the richness of imaginary life compared with the life we have found ourselves unwillingly in the middle of."

"Yes," interrupts another, falling over himself to explain, "but it is the ordinariness of life that makes the writing of the novelette possible, that is the paradox. Imagine (*imagine!*) a life full of the properties of a novelette, how little time there would be for amusing thoughts."

The other china princes mumble in general agreement. "Couldn't agree more, hit the nail on the head, you've said it." Sometimes china princes are grateful for ordinariness, for the small scale of vagabonds, rogues and women, plural and pluperfect.

(The molecules of their speech)

They set out to write
of her but instead

they wrote of
themselves, or was it

she who had written
of them?

(The order of scenes in a monastery: one explanation)

In his youth he once thought to be a Passionist priest, joining an order of men, many of them, for the diversion of certain currents. And these currents would form the fingers of a delta, splayed at all angles, except where his body was, and his spirit would thus be free to be passionate.

But at the last minute, his arms already rushing along the roughness of the holy sleeves, he decided he could not take the vows of the order, but instead made a lifelong promise to make women his passion. Having made this promise, a profession of faith, women became his collected possessions. And everything shall be given for them.

And everything is given and nothing is saved.

(The Passions and Requiems of their salvation)

In the tiny village of Oberammergau, in the Seventeenth Century, the people were threatened by the march of plague across Europe, and they decided that the only way to deliver themselves from the fate of premature death was to petition their maker (who was also, by nature, their destroyer) for a miracle. "The Lord giveth and the Lord taketh away," they said. And they came upon the idea of a Passion play, a play of the Passion of the son of God, to the glory of God.

There followed the furious movement of quills across pages as the script went through its various stages of treatment (as against the weather), scene breakdown (as in atoms separating and coming back together as molecules tight in each other's arms), and draft after draft until

Also songs on the subject of Song

Carroccio

page 57

there was one final draft and this draft, it was said, had come directly from God.

There was great casting of characters and learning of lines and sewing of costumes and constructing of sets in the town. Everyone was to take part, from the oldest conglomeration to the newest atom. This was, after all, for the preservation of their lives. And in the preservation of their lives they invested a goodly proportion of their lives.

Finally the day of the performance arrived, and the great day took three days, three days for the Passion of Jesus, according to the inhabitants of Oberammergau. And everything was given for the glory of God, and for the diversion of death.

And although plague continued to ravage every other town in Europe, Oberammergau remained unscathed. The disease was diverted around it like the miraculous forking of a river. And ever since, the Passion play has been performed regularly, before an audience of thousands watching the upkeep of this spell.

(A foreboding: after Viscount Grey of Falloden)

The lamps are going out
all over Europe;
we shall not
see them lit again
in our lifetime.

(Secular monody, or abandoning the Virgin: after the *Oxford Companion*)

Following in the footsteps of the Eleventh Century goliards — footloose students and errant clerics — jongleurs left their homes and toured the countryside. They sang songs on the subject of wine and women; also songs on the subject of song.

These songs, instead of being taken from Gregorian chant as had been the fashion, were newly composed especially for the performances. The words of the verses were not of the liturgy, but of the worldliness of men who had abandoned the Word. They were, however, in the language of the Church, that is, Latin, and even monks had cause to employ them, singing quietly these Latin profanities to *conduct* a priest from one side of the altar to the other in the course of the Mass.

The secular song was therefore called *conductus*. And sacred and profane, the difference between them was often a sameness.

There were also songs sung in the vernacular, narrative poems of epic proportions. The favourite of these was the *chanson de geste* and the favourite *chanson de geste* was *La Chanson de Roland*. And these were sung often to a repeated melodic formula, which more than likely had its beginnings in plainsong.

And so secular was Latin and sacred was vernacular and vernacular was secular and Latin was sacred. The Church said all roads lead to Gregory and all notes lead to Rome, where music was collected by writing it down, after Gregory. But the secular songs were not notated, or rarely, and so they remained the possessions of worldliness. They were sung by one voice, accompanied by instruments, jugglers and dancing bears. And because they were of a single voice, and because they were, by their subject, profane, they went by the name of secular monody.

The Cult of the Virgin had just about outlived its usefulness.

(To wake in the dark)

Sharing a bed with her limbs they awake one morning to find an eyelash, hers, beside them on the pillow, the woman curled towards them, sleeping. They watch for a moment the to-ing and fro-ing of her eyes beneath their fine membranes of skin, and it is as if they travel back and forth on a bus to a factory for a fortnight's work in quick succession. These are her dreams. China princes, having laid down their heads on this pillow, find themselves encased in her dreams with her. How ordinary it is there! How much they would like their own dream!

"Thank goodness there's more than one of us to cope with it all!" remarks one china prince, and the others all sigh, "Yes, thank goodness!" in unison. But not so loud as to wake her. ("Oh my collapsible dream!")

They are bored, china princes, with the interior of her eyelids, covered with the intricacies of the Sistine ceiling, bombarded with notes from a choir of counter-tenors engaged by the Vatican. China princes see a dream confined to the makings of a bed, and it is unbearable.

"Untenable!"

"We simply cannot live it."

"And that's the end of the matter."

Upon this thought, but against the homing pigeons of their desire, they step over the curve of an eyelash.

They have left.

It is cold. How cold they are! In the cold their hearts are impassioned, though their bodies have barely a movement.

Their first escapade is to go to the typewriter (the same typewriter that once typed an eyelash; they comment on the irony quietly among themselves) where for a good while they tap out a pattern. This portion has nothing whatever to do with their lives, and that is why it amuses them so much.

"People used to write novels about life," remarks one china prince, the one making the coffee, "and now everyone is writing novels about novels." Here he jumps up on the table with as much agility as his china limbs will allow. "Let us write our lives about the novelette!"

The other china princes would cheer and clap, but they don't want to wake the woman. They continue with the story, which is quieter.

Looking up momentarily as dawn begins to break, they discover themselves in the Dark Ages, wondering how many angels can dance on the head of a pin, which is the current obsession. They smile. This is very much to their liking. They would rather wonder than know, especially where angels are concerned. They write it all down quickly, a little guiltily, before the woman might wake and want to know what's going on.

"*Know!*" explodes a china prince. "Bah!"

A tear escapes him, and indeed all the china princes dab surreptitiously at their eyes.

There is, between the Dark Ages and the Age of Enlightenment, this thing called the Middle Ages, but china princes wonder what lies between darkness and light, between C and E-flat, between a man and a woman. How ecstatic it is to wonder together!

Having left the woman's dream, they throw a few things hurriedly into boxes, arrange for carrier pigeons, and go cloaked by the massed darks of the Dark Ages. They embark on their adventures, which would be very humdrum were it not for the novelette and the life they have there. If it weren't for the *Ficta* the tedium of their lives would drive them to distraction.

At the precise moment of their departure they look back and see the woman confined to the small curves of her sleep.

"What was that?" asks a jumpy china prince.

Just as they looked there was a slight movement, a bulging of the parentheses, the turning over of a dream disturbed in its sleep.

(The last minstrel, his lay)

Why do they go? Because their imagination is a field of minstrels. Why are their imaginations so? Because they wear Chinese sleeves and she has ironed them all carefully.

(*De* dream of a woman)

She was dreaming and of what she was dreaming she will tell you in due course, as soon as she has remembered it. What she does remember about this dream is that suddenly there was no dream. The dream had left.

"Good riddance," she said sleepily.

Then there was a great pull upon her, a pull in the middle of her body, where many things reside, organs and breath and where, for instance, love might be. And she was pulled excruciatingly, achingly, by the sucking action of this departure, the departure of winds, moods, an Aeolian harp hanging desultorily in the bough of a tree.

(*Te Deum* of Mozart)

At the age of twenty-three, much travelled and feted throughout his childhood and adolescence, Mozart found himself back home in Salzburg, reluctantly accepting the post of organist at the cathedral. He was in love with a woman, Aloysia, in Paris, and he was taken with the musical styles of Paris, and he would far rather have had Aloysia and Paris than a fussy employer in the backwaters of Salzburg.

He had tasted the delights of larger fields, as a musical prodigy taking Europe by storm. He had played for emperors and he had composed for empresses. He had astonished everyone by scribbling down from memory, upon one hearing in the Sistine Chapel, a *tenebrae* the Vatican had jealously guarded for centuries. At Salzburg, however, his duties were to produce small plain works to the glory of God and to the taste of the Archbishop. Now the Archbishop did not enjoy embellishment in music, nor indeed excess of any kind. He would have been more at home as a Presbyterian, but that persuasion did not exist then. Poor Archbishop. And poor Mozart! With his penchant for ornaments and his predilection for Aloysia, he found his life quite ruled by tedium. He broke out where he could. He snuck in trills and turns, hoping the Archbishop wouldn't notice. And while he composed the small works required of him — a quartet here, a motet there, a *Te Deum* — he dreamed elsewhere and he composed elsewhere, writing an opera secretly by candlelight for a distant patron, and concocting excuses to visit Paris as often as possible.

But on one such occasion his alibi fell through, and Mozart was found out. The Archbishop, who had become increasingly annoyed at the absences of his organist and his frequent disappearances into the intervals between notes, instructed the court chamberlain to kick Mozart down the stairs. The court chamberlain, summoning the necessary display of temper, did so, soundly. And Mozart, picking himself up from the bottom of the staircase, hurled his most recent manuscript at the Archbishop, yelling at the top of his voice, "You can stick your *Te Deum!*" And he left Salzburg never to return.

As for the woman, Aloysia of Paris, sadly she did not reciprocate his affection, but happily Mozart married her sister, Constanze.

(*Cori spezzati,* or divided choirs)

"T for church," said a little girl being wheeled past St Patrick's in her pushchair.

China princes are inside praying for their various shapes and sizes. They must maintain them at all costs. Also the sounds they make. A sound made in a church on a winter's afternoon is not at all transitory, according to china princes. The sound of a soul, its waves, will travel for ever and ever, having everlasting life — provided there are no obstacles in its path to absorb and deaden them. China princes are praying for a clear path from this world to the next.

Ceremonial china vestments hang to air in a corner of the sacristy while the priest is engaged in an afternoon tea ceremony in the kitchen. He kneels on a mat, taking tea.

In the church, similarly in their sleeves and left to their own devices, china princes pray mysteries of the rosary, a plea to the Blessed Virgin, for whom they have a special devotion. They are members of a cult. Between mysteries they throw toast in the aisles. They leap and chant.

A statue of the cult figure stands to one side of the altar. In other recesses about the church are an assortment of major saints made of plaster. On the ceiling are plaster angels, calves of butter studded with jewels, marzipan lilies, doves of ice, hedges like dancing bears, icing swans, and minor saints in the shape of saints, only smaller than life. How they love life! China princes recall that everything is the shape of its own molecular structure.

China princes reflect that perhaps they should take a leaf from the paper-thin gilt that covers the diadems of the saints, especially the holy aura surrounding the head of the Virgin. How beautiful she is! And how tragic the circumstances of her life on Earth! If only they could be like her. How happy they would be!

Alas, confined to their earthly bodies, china princes pray for a good harvest of sackbuts, that they may sing and dance and make music in a manner befitting the Holy Trinity. They hum a triad to themselves and it echoes all the way up to the alpine heights of the ceiling. C, E-flat, G for Gabrieli.

Gabrieli and Gabrieli, father and son, composers of Venice, considered two choirs superior to one. They wrote music for the divided choirs, suspended aloft, in the Church of St Mark, to be accompanied by a consort of instruments. Venice, unlike Rome, allowed instruments to be heard to the glory of God.

And the music shall be tossed from one loft to another, *Kyrie eleison, Christe eleison,* a question, an answer for the Ordinary of the Mass. (Gertrude Stein wrote, *What is the answer? In that case, what is the question?*)(And a soul in a church makes the sound of a soul in a church, said John Cage.)

(In the interval between Middle C and E-flat)

It is minor and therefore dolorous, neither light nor dark. In this space of the drawn breath, the poised finger, the crook'd bow, is a woman selling icecreams from a tray tied around her neck. As in dreams, the intervals between notes could seem like a very long time when you are in them. It is impossible to tell how long they will take and there must be something to keep people amused.

But the fact is, the woman is also the director of the production. She is an *auteur* usherette. She wants to do everything: to direct, to show people to their seats, then sell them trumpets which have been muted with plugs of icecream to keep down the noise in the theatre.

China princes, licking rhythmically, find themselves staring into the electric eyes of a pair of roaring lions which flank the stage. China princes are jostled by a throng of bodies whose movements are sliced by the minute trembling of dimmed lights. These bodies have the appearance of china, should a collection of ornaments have taken it into their heads to walk across a room. China princes, remembering their days in the factory and the vow of china they made there regarding their bodies, feel quite at home.

There is much discussion about the note that has just been performed — the quality of is production, its timbre, and of course its extraordinary pitch. It was of such *pitch*. Reviews appear in newspapers sold by children calling on street corners. An accolade. The beauty of that note! "The note just spent was of such beauty even the wind was in awe of it," wrote Ernest Newman.

The audience, waving their programs in a friendly gesture towards heat, speculate on the approach of the next note, an E-flat. How will it do on opening night?

(And where do they come from, and where do they go?)

An *entre-acte* of angels dances in the foyer. They all wear lime-green miniskirts and hoop earrings, and their movements are one. They lip-sync "Needles and Pins" in perfect unison.

"What is it keeps them in time?" asks a bystander, noticing that there is no music in this interval between notes.

"Ah!" replies a music student, straightening her spectacles on the bridge of her nose. "Just as the conductor imagines the graffiti he scrawls in the air, so the performers — and often the audience as well — imagine they see a conductor."

A woman, lately caught in the revolving doors leading from the streetmap into the foyer, now finding herself negotiating the sliding doors of the crowd as she tries to enter the theatre proper, thinks she sees a man of her acquaintance out of the corner of her eye. In the next moment her eyes are drawn as if by force towards him, as are her limbs, her hair and the loose ends of her clothing. Her scarf flies horizontal like that of the *Petit Prince*. She seems to have stepped into a magnetic field, or an alarming vacuum created by the man's body.

Just as she is about to disappear with bits of fluff, cigarette butts and icecream wrappers, never to be seen again, she sees another man, exactly the same as the first, and towards this man too she is inextricably drawn, and now her limbs, her hair, her clothing set off in his direction. Presently, another man, just the same as the first two — she is drawn to him also, and then another, and another. In the end the woman counts seventeen men, all looking like the man of her acquaintance, and all having this suction effect on her. She assumes every man in the world looks like this, and acts upon her like this — at least, every man likely to find himself in the interval between Middle C and E-flat — and there is no earthly good trying to tell them apart. She comes to the conclusion that this pull in every direction is how the earth remains on its axis.

This thought has just occurred to her when she is disturbed by a hush, a remarkable hush by John Cage. The E-flat is about to begin.

And that is the end of the interval.

(Hildegard learning the language of a dove)

She took instruction in Latin from a monk, Volmar, whose pearls of wisdom fell in decades from his quill. But Hildegard, once an attentive student of all things, now began indulging in the habit of daydreaming.

Seeing her so obviously distracted, Volmar asked, "What is it? What unminds thee so, sister?"

Hildegard, though she opened her mouth to reply, could not summon any words to her lips. Jutta looked on and exchanged anxious glances with the monk.

Then Volmar said, "I know what it is!", holding his finger aloft to signal an idea.

"What?" whispered Jutta.

"Hildegard is learning Latin from the Holy Ghost."

"The Holy Ghost himself?" marvelled Jutta, and blessed herself.

"The Holy Ghost via the voice of a dove who speaks into her ear," said Volmar.

Though he continued to visit the cell, he now left instruction to the dove. Notwithstanding this divine intervention, Hildegard's command of Latin remained unscholarly.

Presently she took sick and she took to her bed. It was a mysterious illness of undiagnosed symptoms. Aches and pains, and ague and a racing heart. Volmar was barred entry to the cell by the nun, Richardis, who had come as a nursemaid. And attended by Richardis and the supposed ringing of Latin in her ears, Hildegard lay back and contemplated tremulously the ceiling of her cell. And there she saw her wonderings; but kept them fiercely to herself, and they consumed her like the illness that wracked her body. And she came to know her wonderings as she knew the back of her hand, or a streetmap of stars, the order of the Mass, or a sequence of dreams. When Volmar addressed her in Latin, from time to time, she could not answer, did not appear to understand. Volmar said it was merely the mysterious workings of the dove, but Hildegard knew she could not say anything if it was not of the astonishments. And although the rhythm of her life kept strictly to self-denial, contemplation and prayer, she knew (*knew*) that one day she would burst into free verse.

(All in good time)

She has not left her bed
but her reason
a woman, madness, her
passion cycling halfway
between Heaven and Earth.
She has imagined his

imaginings marked on a streetmap of the universe
the way the universe is:
an ellipse with protrusions
stars falling, angels, musical
notes from the Vatican City
the inside the same as the
outside
the way it all proceeds
into the next world
before she has seen
anything of it.

(Dominions to sleep under)

Though princes, they are very poor. They spend most of their time in the Auckland Domain. It is cold and they have on everything they own, not that that is very much; their china hats and coats and their imported Chinese sleeves, a waistcoat with china buttons and a scene of fox and hounds. Every morning there is a scramble to be first dressed in what most becomes them, and then it becomes them.

The leaves are falling from the trees. Everywhere there are leaves, and china princes, having no sackbut to play on (having buried the sackbut), amuse themselves and also keep warm by sweeping up leaves. If they weren't stern with themselves they could easily make this their life's work. There is an obsessive nature to these leaves, and also it is always winter so there are always dead leaves. It is winter because they are dressed in their china garments, pink, yellow and blue, and they wear these because it is winter. That is the way it is.

And that is why there are so many leaves which must be collected. To stop themselves running across a lawn to pick up a single leaf freshly fallen on a patch just swept, china princes rest on benches facing the other way, away from the bareness of winter trees, towards the Memorial

Museum, where there is an exhibition they have yet to visit.

Oh it is cold. How cold it is! — though a dove flew in through an ear and out through a mouth, warming a mind momentarily with the fluttering of its feathers.

It is very cold in the Domain and for a long time china princes sit looking at marble statues and looking remarkably like them. It is cold, but that is just as well because china princes have nothing on underneath their china hats and coats and their sleeves and their waistcoats, and so they cannot take them off — this is in the middle of the Auckland Domain and people are dotted about everywhere on their lunch hours. And also china princes' hats and coats etc. are made of china and there is difficulty in taking them off, in fact, it is impossible to do so without injury.

As it happens, the park benches are relieved that china princes sit for such a long time because benches are modest and they have nothing on underneath china princes.

They have no thought for a woman going about the ordinariness of her business, but day and night she wonders about the adventures of a band of men.

(An exhibition of warmth)

A billboard outside the Memorial Museum declares that everything in the exhibition is of a wonderful temperature, rarely seen before. China princes, having seen everything in this world but wanting to see more, come one afternoon to gaze into the glass cases of rare, warm objects, and they can hardly contain their astonishment.

(The condensation of shadows)

There was once St Hildegard of the Twelfth Century and of the walling up of nuns and of the Council of How Many Angels Can Dance on the Head of a Pin, and of the beating of her dreams against the ceiling of her cell, turned into visions.

When she could stand it no longer, the ecstasy of seeing the despair of silence, she sat down and in a frenzy wrote *The Bright Cloud and the Shadow*, in unscholarly Latin; and the text was immediately transcribed by Volmar and illuminated by another monk in the abbey. Their three sleeves slid across three pages.

(Their prayers answered)

A consort of sackbuts
adorns a tree, china princes

reach up and pick them
persimmon apart from

the sound they make
that of an ornament. Grace.

Now they each have a sackbut!
Jongleurs!

(After Hildegard: *The Bright Cloud and the Shadow*)

Then I saw
as it were a great throng of living
torches, very bright
kindled by a bolt of fiery lightning
from which they acquired
a glowing splendour.
And behold! there appeared
a lake, very broad and deep
with a mouth like a well
belching forth
fiery smoke and a terrible
stench. From the lake too came
a hideous cloud of mist

*which billowed out to touch
something like a vein
with deceiving eyes. Through it
the foul cloud breathed upon a shining cloud
filled with stars upon
stars, which issued
from the beautiful form of
a man in a region
of light. Thus
the foul cloud cast the shining cloud
and the human form
out of that region. After this
a luminous splendour surrounded the place
and all the elements of the world
which had formerly lain in great peace
became turbulent and displayed
frightful terrors.*

III

The Sadness and Dancing of a Woman Entertaining Her Lover and the Thoughts in His Head

From then on there were choirs of angels falling from the sky; for if the inside of St Hildegard's head were the same as the outside, then the inside of the universe was the same as what lay beyond its protrusions.

(Dividing the String: the first adventure of the jongleurs)

Their name is Land or the laying on of hands and they have nothing to their name apart from their home in the Hokianga. Because they have nothing their house is of corrugated cloud and there is no need for windows as the walls are a much more realistic image of the sky than a sky seen through glass. They once lived in suburban Auckland and they found, on looking out the windows of their house, that their gaze went all the way to the extent of the universe and did not return.

On the Land they are growing vegetables of every shape, size and flavour imaginable. Also they have invented some. Sackbuts, for instance, hang from the trees in winter — which it is, it is always winter. Tubers they have trained to send their roots towards a pot swinging above a fire. One Land translates the *Tao Te Ching* from this warmth. Between them they have found that many Lands make light work.

A spring runs the length of their property, the length of the universe, or a diagram of it they have drawn using every available perch. Just as the city of Dunedin was laid out as a replica of the city of Edinburgh, regardless of hills and dales, resulting in a peculiar turn, steepness and camber of street, so the universe superimposed on the Land has a particular quirkiness.

Now that they have their sackbuts, china princes take up their long lost profession of jongling. Following a map they have inside their heads, they find themselves there among the landed Lands, who have nevertheless renounced worldly goods.

"Good day, we are jongleurs," they say.

"Oh!" exclaim the Lands. "We could do with a tune. It's been so long."

"Tunes we have aplenty," say the jongleurs, fanning open the copious pages of the *chansonnier*.

"Come in, come in," invite the Lands, and jongleurs enter the corrugated building.

In an episode without possessions, jongleurs have arrived with boxes of their belongings transported by carrier pigeon. The Lands are aghast. "So many worldly goods!" they exclaim.

Jongleurs explain that these are the things they threw together hurriedly on the morning they embarked on their adventures.

The Lands nod doubtfully.

But what was it that so urgently required packing anyway? the jongleurs wonder. What could they not live without? They cannot for the life of them remember. These things they have not laid eyes on for quite some time and that, according to the Lands, is the measure of their usefulness.

"The laying on of eyes," say the Lands sagely.

An angel is the jongleurs' heaviest possession, but the Lands, having no possessions to their name, wonder how many angels can dance on the head of a pin. At night they wonder at length, because there is no electricity and the women cannot see to sew (nor do they dare sew during the day for fear of disturbing these angels and going about with them clinging to the tips of their fingers). Because they cannot see the heads of pins, the Lands have no doubt that one day they will discover how many angels dance upon them.

An angel is their heaviest possession

XXII   Ciufoli Pastorali   Page 74

"It is not a question of counting but of wondering," they say.

Then the Lands quickly send away the boxes, but laying their eyes on the sackbuts, they rejoice, crying, "This is indeed the Middle Ages!" (The first time they saw a Coke can it blew them away.) "How about a tune?"

Jongleurs sing and dance and play their sackbuts for the entertainment of the Lands. They perform airs and graces and *chansons des gestes* from the *chansonnier*, but embellished beyond recognition.

(And word travels quickly, via a spy in the Hokianga, to the South of France and the dour troubadour, hearing of the spectacle made of his songs, sets out immediately for the Land.)

And a great company of notes flies up into the sky and encounters, quite by chance, a sleeping woman. She has just been flung from a crate, is tumbling in a wide arc, and she looks as if she might be about to come to her senses. At the sight of her the jongleurs' instruments fall from their lips, their voices flee them.

"What is it?" ask the Lands, startled by the sudden silence.

"Oh," stammer the jongleurs, "it's just the sight of our possessions, up there, you know, on the loose, so to speak."

"Ah," nod the Lands, but they shake their heads among themselves. Such attachment to material possessions is quite beyond them. Looking up into the universe they have acquired — a universe of small lands and vast sky, a sky much larger than the space above Land — they glimpse what they think is the shape of a woman, but disregard it, instead seeing teatrays departing.

One Land observes: "Possessions in search of a possessor, or of the possessed."

The jongleurs once more put their sackbuts to their lips and try to blow but it is as if they have sucked lemons and no sound is created.

(The Cult figurine)

Like a particular particle in the universe
she does not exist
until he thinks about her.
Her limbs and those of a tree
are bare. It is always
winter. Her coldness
that of a china figurine
could be warmed
by his breath
in her ear
if only he would make a visitation
upon her
but she has imagined
he does not and so
he does not.

(A hindrance)

There was once St Hildegard of the Twelfth Century and of the walling up of nuns and of divine inspiration, her free verse and the excesses of her plainsong, and of the Council of How Many Angels Can Dance on the Head of a Pin, and of the Gift of Tears, and of her hospitality to a band of jongleurs who happened to find themselves at her abbey between the hours of daylight and daylight.

Her fame was spreading across Europe. The hierarchy of the Church — the Pope of the day, who by this time was Pope Gelasius II, and the anti-pope, Gregory VIII, and the Holy See and the bishops and archbishops — having once turned a blind eye to the weakness of women, now discovered that with regard to the teachings of the Church, whereby the lowly shall be exalted, women had a particular advantage. And they listened with the rapt attention of the blind to the astonishing female allegorist.

And the mystery of the rosaries of birds cast in the sky above the monastery of St Disibod's was now explained. It was not the abbot's piety that manufactured them, rather their nests were flushed from the gutterings of Hildegard's robes.

Within the walls of the monastery there was much to-ing and fro-ing on account of the visionary Hildegard. And Hildegard, no longer solitary but attended by her favoured nun, Richardis, and her favoured monk, Volmar, lay back on her narrow bed and struck the pose normally associated with the state of ecstasy; and she related the visions appearing on the ceiling of her cell which, miraculously, were in accordance with the liturgical year, all seasons bar winter.

And as the tears slid down the walls of her cell they were mopped up by a child who would grow into the Caretaker Pope, but was yet a choirboy.

Young women wanting to join the order of Hildegard, to live a life shuffled into the orderliness of allegory, came from all directions to follow the paths of her tears.

A band of jongleurs, roaming the countryside in the South of France, got word of Hildegard, and word is deed, and they set out for Mount St Disibod, where they presented themselves at the door of the monastery, together with their sackbuts, etc., and began to play.

Hildegard, disturbed in the middle of a vision of angels clinging to the tips of the fingers of nuns weaving tapestries for the altar of the Blessed Sacrament, paused when she heard the extraordinary sound of seventeen jongleurs playing together, and recognised that these jongleurs were not part of her vision. They were very real; or so she thought, going to peer through the grille in the wall.

And so they thought, jongleurs, producing a song from the budget of songs the dour troubadour had given them, profusely ornamented and four-beats-to-the-measure.

Hildegard asked Richardis, Elisabeth (a protegee) and Volmar, clustered about her at the grille, "Who are those jongleurs who have discovered winter?"

But no one could tell her, for the Abbot had turned the jongleurs away, branding them heretics on account of their Common Time.

Hearing this, Hildegard was outraged. "It is unchristian!" she cried. "I don't know why I stay in this place."

Whereupon Volmar said, "Hildegard, don't throw the baby out with the bathwater!"

Hildegard nodded, then narrowed her eyes. "But mark my words, there will be winter in this monastery if I have to tear off the roof myself to let it in." And at that moment was born the avant garde. So Hildegard pinpointed it in retrospect. She was before and she was, after all, Garde for short, and later she named the movement after everything that had happened and everything that was to happen, and after herself.

And the choirboy with the moppy broom smiled quietly to himself, inspired by the allegorist.

The jongleurs left the monastery door hurriedly without argument. You can't argue with zealots, and anyway they were eager to continue with their adventures, of which A Hindrance was not one.

(*The Four Seasons,* a concerto)

The excellence of the musicianship of the girls of the *Ospedale della Pieta*, Venice, was much in demand, although no one had ever laid eyes on the girls themselves. At Sunday performances they sat demurely screened by walls of silk (the strands of their violins passing through silk and therefore made silken) while the musical director, Antonio Vivaldi, conducted within full view of the audience. The difference was one of gender, the sameness was music.

And for the entertainment of the audience, but also of the girls, sadly orphaned and in need of families, Vivaldi had composed quantities of concerti, one after the other, like the planting of a forest of family trees. And the concerti were strong and lush and beautiful, and the girls, unloved, fell instantly in love with them. For if they were starved for love they would give love; that is one of the paradoxes of this world. And that explained why the famed Sunday performances were so imbued with passion.

Vivaldi had been ordained a priest but could not celebrate Mass on account of being stricken with asthma, doubt, one or the other. His difficulty with breathing was construed as a vote of no confidence in the earthly manifestations of God. He was thus appointed musical director of the *Ospedale*. Music was considered only halfway to God. At the *Ospedale* he composed program music, his concerti painting pictures of seasons, moods, loves, using the vibrant strokes of violins.

His concerto most liked by the girls and audience alike was *The Four Seasons: winter, winter, winter and winter*, a manifestation of the coldness of birds and the bareness of trees and the requiem masses of clouds. And the girls played it with even more passion than usual and the audience rose to its feet to applaud, and Vivaldi thought he must have done something right with so many winters. And he pondered, was there not always this loss, a bareness, a sadness, heard but not seen? and he thought that that was what he had captured in the concerto.

And the girls of the *Ospedale della Pieta*, their passion boarding notes to pass through the pure silk where they themselves would never go, were heard but not seen in its rendering.

(The lure of the Cult)

Out of season
the most desired
season.

(A wintering of monks)

And seeing the continual stream of condensation that ran down the walls of the cell of the visionary, the religious remarked that winter had indeed come to St Disibod's. And winter stayed and winter stayed, and for many years there was nothing but winter.

(Profession of Sleeves: the second adventure of the jongleurs)

The price of fish is nothing they are concerned with, but the fishing of fish is the constant delight of a group of monks. For other religions in the monastery it is the gathering of apples, the worshipping of persimmon lighting a tree, the kneading of dough and the rising in the dark for the singing of praises. Their prayers at this hour are an eclipse of the sun.

All in their long sleeves the monks make themselves like each other, both ways: "I like you," even though they may not (this is their philosophy) and "I am like you," even though they are not at all alike underneath their sleeves.

But that is the point of it, dressing this way, all the same. The point of a pin is, by dressing the same they have exposed all their differences. Their sandals are similar but their feet are different. They all have beards but some are black and some are white, some are silent and some are muttered into.

The monks put their hands into their sleeves fossicking for a meal and a night's rest for a band of jongleurs who, they notice appreciatively, look exactly alike. The jongleurs say they have travelled a great distance to be here, according to a map of the universe, or of their heads. ("The inside of our heads is the same as the outside, you know." The monks nod their approval.) They have weathered furies and passions, they have traversed a ravine of the nature of sound.

In gratitude for the meal of bread and wine, jongleurs take up their voices and their instruments and they begin to sing, with accompaniment, a *chanson* of romantic love plucked from the Age of Chivalry like the harvesting of an apple and stored to last the whole winter, and its notes are of such beauty that they inspire obsession. Once heard, the hearer, professing love, has no thought but to follow these notes to the end of the Earth. Their lure could persuade even a monk to abandon the monastery and go after them.

But before the jongleurs have got more than a few bars into the *chanson* they are silenced by a serious bustling among the older monks, who have each taken a vow of the absence of speech, as is the custom, these vows stretching like soundwaves or tsunamis from this world to the next; also a vow of poverty; and another of abstinence from the pleasures of the fourth beats of measures, which is of course the metre of the *chanson*. Jongleurs protest that the *chanson* was once a hymn to the Blessed Virgin Mary; it has been converted. But the monks indicate with a shaking of their heads, which in turn causes their sleeves to tremble, that this is little to the point. The point is, there are many points of view but there is only one view, and the heretical *chanson* will not be heard in this monastery.

(But the dour troubadour is already hurrying across on his way from the Lands'.)

Later, one monk explains to the jongleurs in hushed tones, lest a soundwave overhear, that though other orders may have gone the liberal way there is no room for romance in this cloister. They are a state of individuals. "Nevertheless, many hands make a light meal," he murmurs offering, in all hospitality, a profusion of the fruits of their sameness.

(The state of Bingen)

There is Bingen and there is not Bingen, and not Bingen was for many years what Hildegard was.

Despite the following of young women who came to winter at her abbey — protusions like biddybids which clung to the hem of her gown as she swept along the corridors of the monastery — despite these numbers there was no place for Hildegard to go where she could have her own dominion. She therefore petitioned Kuno, the Abbot of St Disibod's, for a convent to be built at Rupertsburg, opposite Bingen am Rhein, a site revealed to her in a vision — to no avail.

But to know a veil, as Hildegard did, her Benedictine habit, is to know perseverance; one knows it as one knows a vow, in the biblical sense. And Hildegard, her following continuing to gather about the nether regions of her habit, stayed on at St Disibod's, but she did not stay silent on the matter of Bingen.

(Only joking: after the *Oxford Companion*)

The *chanson de geste*, performed with great gusto in the Middle Ages by itinerant musicians, employed the same tunes that had for centuries sung the praises of the Blessed Virgin Mary, since the gathering of wide sleeves denoting the Cult. The Virgin had remained blessed, while the melodies had become profane things, with four beats per bar, and many worldly instruments in the role of companion/help.

After a little time, no more than two centuries, there was a blurring — as if the focus-puller differentiating between the distances of Dark, Middle and Enlightenment had allowed his clarity to lapse — and the tunes were strung together into decades, and the decades into mysteries stretching away into the dimness of both past and future. And the songs were performed with drama and dancing and other sorrows inbetween like knots in a piece of string separating beads. These progressions were the first operas.

Presently in Italy, among the emigres of strung-together *chansons*, there occurred a great schism in the matter of Plot and Passion; of what happens, and how what happens is received. And a great ravine opened up between the two, with Plot taking plainness and Passion being left with the uncontrollable excess of emotion — the heights of ecstasy, the depths of despair. And oh how sorry Passion was that it found itself on that side of the ravine!

Plot was meantime schooled in the art of reduction by a band of musicians eager to get on with *why we are here*. They found themselves hindered by the demands of the story — that it must be *told*. And they decided that the story could be rendered in half-minute segments of many syllables of text sung very fast on the same note, or thereabouts, as a voice running on the spot, or Gregorian Chant. This practice they called recitative.

And that was what was done, and the single voice of the recit. (as is was affectionately known) told everything as fast as was humanly possible given the constraints of tongues and teeth. Like the clattering of keys on a typewriter, it could only go so fast (and that was why awkward reaches were built into the typewriter keyboard, to slow down the typist to the speed of the machine, but that is another story). And telling everything included arrivals, departures, secrets, predictions, intentions and intrigue; everything, that is, apart from the havoc these acts wreak on the soul; everything apart from love and hatred, ecstasy and despair.

And for love and hatred, etc., Plot stood respectfully aside for the long moment of an aria. And the aria had no responsibility to the story, only to passion. And such was the aria's beauty, and such were the pourings into it and out of it, notes returning from soffits in full regalia, that audiences rose to their feet and cheered and clapped, warming the palms of their hands, their lifelines; and the layered volcano sands of their various past loves and hatreds, ecstasies and despairs, long dormant, were woken again in the darkness.

The union of the Cult of the Virgin and the laity was thus consummated.

From then on, following the establishment of recitative and the adoration of the aria, what fell between stories assumed the utmost importance. The moment of feeling was magnified, while that of *what happened* was viewed through the wrong end of a telescope. And that is why the highlights of operas, collected on cassette tapes and CDs, are utterly devoid of narrative.

(If you look in one place long enough you will see a woman)

Every three minutes a comet travelling at high speed, the speed of height, passes every single point in the sky, but no one bothers to look. And a comet travelling more slowly passes, once every hundred years, a particular point viewed by millions of stargazers saying, "The comet passed in my lifetime!" Yet the appearances are much the same thing, the difference a matter of scale.

A woman in the sky is following a dream she once inhabited.

"Or it inhabited me," she murmurs.

She left her mind to become a heavenly body among the peripatetic attentions of stars, and tipped a planet off its axis quite by accident on her way past. As a consequence a mode went awry (the tempering of everything!) and a mood was ruffled and the wind was set askew.

"How sad these changes are!" says the woman breathlessly.

She is lost. Looking down to try to find her bearings from the positions of the streetlamps in January, concentrating on the same spot for several minutes, she sees a band of men pass by. By the stiffness of their bodies and their glossiness, they appear to be made of china embellished here and there with gold dip. Their clothes belie noble beginnings which they are trying earnestly to conceal by carrying sackbuts, etc., like common jongleurs. As the woman watches, the jongleurs cross the Channel to England where there are dancing bears in the shape of clipped hedges, jesters with bells dangling from their hats and from the tips of their fingers. And she is filled with the most unaccountable sense of *once she was there and now she is here* — and the possessions are there, and possession is nine-tenths of the law. She is left with a tithe, what Hildegard was, the tenth child given to the Church in gratitude to God for the bounty of children, the other nine of them.

Meanwhile the jongleurs, setting foot on English soil for the first time, find that St Augustine has been there before them, accompanied by a flock of forty monks, messengers of Gregory the Great, their purpose to convert the heathen. When Gregory himself visited England and saw for the first time blond heads, he said, *"They are called Angles. It is well, for they have the faces of angels and as such should be the co-heirs of the angels of Heaven."* And in his path

Augustine had left a trail of notes leading to a multitude of churches and abbeys all over the land.

Baffled by this profusion of straight Roman roads — whole stavesful, five lanes all leading in the same direction, to Rome — jongleurs squint up into the night sky, perchance to be guided by the heavens in January, and they see a small tailed star, blurred, and on account of the blurring they think to look twice, but when they look back it is gone.

And when they look back at the Earth they find the notes are gone and the churches and abbeys are gone. There is only what has been filigreed between, for ornament.

(The Splitting of Hairs: the third adventure of the jongleurs)

A peer of the realm, of this morning, or of the middle of the Seventeenth Century, has a large garden with an herbaceous border, a maze, and also a vacancy for an ornamental hermit. For the past seven years a solitary man with only a beard for company, to mutter into, has lived at the bottom of the garden, dressed in rags, sleeping under trees, and eating the plate of food put out for him in the middle of each afternoon. An ornament, he spoke to no one. He struck poses to please the peer and any of the guests who came down to the edge of the New Formalist garden hoping to catch sight of him in the arms of a dancing bear.

It is the law that after seven years as an ornament, the hermit is provided with a hut and a living for the rest of his days, and for the rest of his days he may speak to anyone he so wishes. But usually after seven years' silence the solitary man finds that speech has outlined its usefulness.

Because they are quite polite and display a certain monkishness, also because of an ability to play the sackbut and to make china roses which the peer thinks might look well in his rose arbour in the winter, also because they stand one behind the other so he thinks there is only one of them when they apply for job, the jongleurs are invited by the peer of the realm to become his new ornamental hermit.

On a winter afternoon they move to the bottom of the garden, their possessions following by homing-pigeons finding their next home. It is cold. Jongleurs find no leaves on the trees, only branches and bleakness. But they are great believers in seasons, especially winter. (It is always winter.)

"See how bare the trees are!" cries one jongleur. "How beautiful they are!"

And the other jongleurs look at the trees and see that they are bare, and indeed more beautiful than they were before.

Presently another jongleur comes over from another part of the garden and says, "Look at the crazy paving, how beautiful it is when it is in that mood." And another says listen to the windchimes, how the wind chimes; and another has heard that the maze is so complicated that peers of the realm have never returned from it.

"They go the same way as younger sons voyaging to the South Seas," says a maudlin jongleur.

While they are unpacking their possessions — pictures, notes, an angel, a dressmaker, the limpness of a woman's clothing left by a bed, and of course the beloved sackbuts of their chosen profession — jongleurs look around the garden and wonder what constitutes the realm.

"What is it made of and what is the matter with it?" they ask each other, going about fingering everything.

They look up at the manor and see that it is made of stone with glass windows, but they can find no stone in the ground, nor the minerals for making glass. Jongleurs spread their hands in gestures of perplexity. The peer of the realm and his friends are evidently making merry, drinking inside and out on the terraces overlooking the garden. But there are no grapes or monks on this property to make wine. Jongleurs wonder if this realm is not what it seems, but something imagined in a far-off land.

Nevertheless they plant their china roses in the rose arbour. The trellis fences cast the pattern of a shadowbox across them, and before long they are feeling very much at home in their ornamental hermitage. They light a fire and dance around it, singing *chansons de gestes* accompanied by their sackbuts, a windfall windchime, and anything else that may have fallen from a tree. They would like it if the peer and his friends would come and listen, and then they would, strictly speaking, be jongling; but then again, they would blow their solitary disguise.

It occurs to each of the china princes, for the first time, that perhaps being singular has its distinct advantages, but nobody mentions it for fear of upsetting the others.

In the course of the proceedings one of the china princes remembers that day is a certain birthday.

"Of course! Silly me. How could I be so *stupid*!" exclaim the other jongleurs, clapping their palms to their brows.

Today is the ninth birthday of the writing of a certain novelette. Jongleurs forgot in the rush, but now they celebrate this great age by making merry all the more. Someone says a dog ages fourteen years in one year, and a novelette's one year is equal to nine human years. This makes this the eighty-first birthday of the novelette, and that requires a speech.

"Speech, speech!" cry the jongleurs.

The most golden of the jongleurs stands on a tree stump and, raising his glass to the stars (his attention taken fleetingly by a comet that he notices seems to be stuck in the sky), he proclaims, "This book is an autobiography! Everything in this book we have thought of ourselves!"

A great cheer goes up and jongleurs dance and sing and play all the harder. With all their carryings on they don't notice that the manor has become silent and is in darkness. They are having such a time of it, jongleurs, that they would not recognise a catastrophe were it to occur to them in their train of thoughts.

(And indeed, the dour troubadour, racing across fields in the dead of night, will shortly descend upon them and snatch back his *chansonnier*.)

The peer of the realm, disturbed in his dreams, sits up in bed and rubs his eyes. He's not sure but he thinks the rowdiness may be the work of the new ornamental hermit. Unbelievable! He gets out of bed and, in his nightshirt, runs down into the rose arbour towards the fire. Seeing there not one but seventeen solitary men, he drives them out of the garden.

The way a windchime
makes wind: the wind
was not there
until a windchime
stopped it in its tracks,
the windchime was not there
until china princes
came to gaze upon it.

(The romance of Beethoven (never married))

He always lived alone but together with his hearing and a piano he kept in the front room. These were like black cats. He composed at first like an ageing Mozart, in Classical style — this in his late teens. His body assumed the pose of Classical statuary, completely absorbed, in a public park.

He courted the piano, paying her every attention, the caress of his fingers, the hissed pencilling of sweet nothings.

"Oh my little pudding! My plump bunch of grapes!"

"Oh!" gasped the piano.

He took the liberty of delivering to her, chords plucked from her own wilderness.

She responded accordingly with oohs and aahs and excited cries, and these glorious sounds came to be known as Beethoven's genius.

His neglected hearing was, of course, jealous but too much in love to pack up and leave. Instead she weathered the ménage à trois. And anyway, as she suspected, the honeymoon was brief between the piano and Beethoven.

As he got older he grew more passionate, but also more moody and difficult to live with, unbearable at certain points in a composition. He threw tantrums. He hurled plates across the room, liking the sound they made when they smashed, he said afterwards by way of apology.

The piano put up with it. "That's all right," she murmured.

The neighbours said she was the classic doormat.

His hearing was more sensitive. She crouched in the corner, trembling and holding her hands over her ears, while Beethoven, unconcerned, composed the program music of trees, pastorals, as was the fashion; their unstable lives filled with loss and the picking up, once again, of the pieces. How blinkered you are! said hearing to herself. He wrote also the program music of his feelings, which in an afternoon could run the whole gamut of the seasons. He was becoming an unashamed Romantic.

Meanwhile Napoleon marched into Russia, leading an army of well-fed troops. It was a popular campaign. Beethoven, for one, was right behind him.

"I'm right behind you, Bonaparte!" he said, while remaining of course at home in Bonn.

But while Napoleon found winter, winter and more winter — the Russians retreating and burning villages in their wake — the symphonies of Beethoven now became staged like the battles the troops would have fought had there been anyone there to fight. For Beethoven there were no such strategical problems as retreat. A leap of faith was as good as a flagged pin in a map. He made large-scale movements from one key to another, and he always won.

In his thirties, a young man no longer but neither an old one, Beethoven discovered that he had difficulty, on occasion, of discerning the answering-back of his beloved — hearing, that is; his piano he still took for granted. Sometimes he saw a note crossing the room on tiptoes which he had not been aware had left the soundboard.

"Yo! Who goes there!" he thundered, but the notes skittered away giggling and whispering about him (he thought) under their breath.

His anger at these notes, escaping without his notice, led him to pound the keyboard violently; although sometimes, planning an ambush, he would construct the most delicate *adagio* in the hope the notes would be lulled for an instant into thinking they could get away with these elopements.

They could not. Beethoven the strategist would see to it that they could not.

(Unto Black Death)

The outpourings of his heart
the inclinations of his body an art
form he has revealed to the woman,
of no such thing of
ordinary things, also, is
one of her titles along with
coloratura soprano and everlasting
princess of everything you can think of.
When he unstops these Passionist
beliefs learned from an order
of priests — it is not just that he thinks
he is in love with her, she is
an article of his faith — she lies
back on her bed together
with a basketful of kittens
her long cigarette trailing
the remains of a novelette
she has imagined, *Musica
Ficta,* meaning beauty
is falseness and things
are not the way they seem
they are only the way they are,
and she invites him to enter
her body through her ear
divine inspiration and also a cloud
encounters a soffit. A moment before
she would not let him inside her
house (she has studied in-

difference). He has noticed a palpable
improvement in the relationship
which swings between them
a hammock one of them one day
will dive into in the arms of another.
Nevertheless clasping
the ornate curves of her
hair and the continuation
of her body from the last time
he touched its recesses
when he discovered that for a moment
he dominated the woman the dominant
thought in his head and was therefore
master of his own thoughts and also
a captive of them,
the china figurines of
courtly love — revisiting
this vision he remembers
the way their souls once
bounced off walls
the ball in her court
or, she thought, in his.

(A Sudden Happiness)

Remember this: that the third is operative, the third is what determines what is major and what is minor, what is happy and what is sad.

Following the entry of the Devil into the Garden, there was the little matter of imperfection in the nature of sound and what must be done about it. (The way atoms have fallen. It is cold. The poet will always be with us.)

A piece of music in a minor key, sadness — when it comes to its conclusion, it was quite natural it should desire a minor chord to finish off, also to finish on, seeing minor was what it was used to and minor was what it had always known. However, as it happens, every note in the entire world contains a *major* third, happiness, in its harmonic series (the harmonic series being the family of tiny notes stretching upwards from the firstborn to the youngest member at the limits of hearing; the little notes that make up a note, give it its timbre). Every single note contains this major third because that is the way God intended it, imbuing sound with his infinite goodness. And also the way Pythagorus imagined it, and therefore, the way it is.

But a major third in a minor key? — Well, of course they clash when sounded together. Oh the difficulty of everything! There is always a problem. Theorists scratched their heads. They put on white coats, held test tubes over Bunsen burners and wrote simultaneous equations for four hands. But all to no avail.

Then one young student, a woman living in penury in a garret overlooking the Seine, did what no one had done since Pythagorus — she took a leap of faith, imagining what might be. She imagined the transmuting of the final minor chord into a major chord, by making the errant minor third into a major third (using, of course, *musica ficta*). And her theory was that if all was major at the end of a piece — the third of the harmonic series, and the third of the chord — then all would be well. Her leap of faith was: Would a major chord sound at home at the end of a minor piece? It had never before been imagined. She tried once and she tried it many times, inserting major thirds and filling her poky garret with a slagheap of discarded minor thirds. But for many months the major third would not *take*.

She had all but exhausted her meagre supply of chords (all she could afford) and was living on six radishes for dinner, when one day, a major third *took*. "I have found it! I have found it!" she said softly to herself. The answer to the riddle of the clashing thirds was indeed the sudden switch at the end of a piece from minor to major. And she tried it once more, and once more it was so; major sounded well after minor. In her excitement she rushed to the window and cried out over the *quartier*, "A sudden happiness! That is the answer!"

And a sudden happiness entered the music of the Church, and indeed the music of all things.

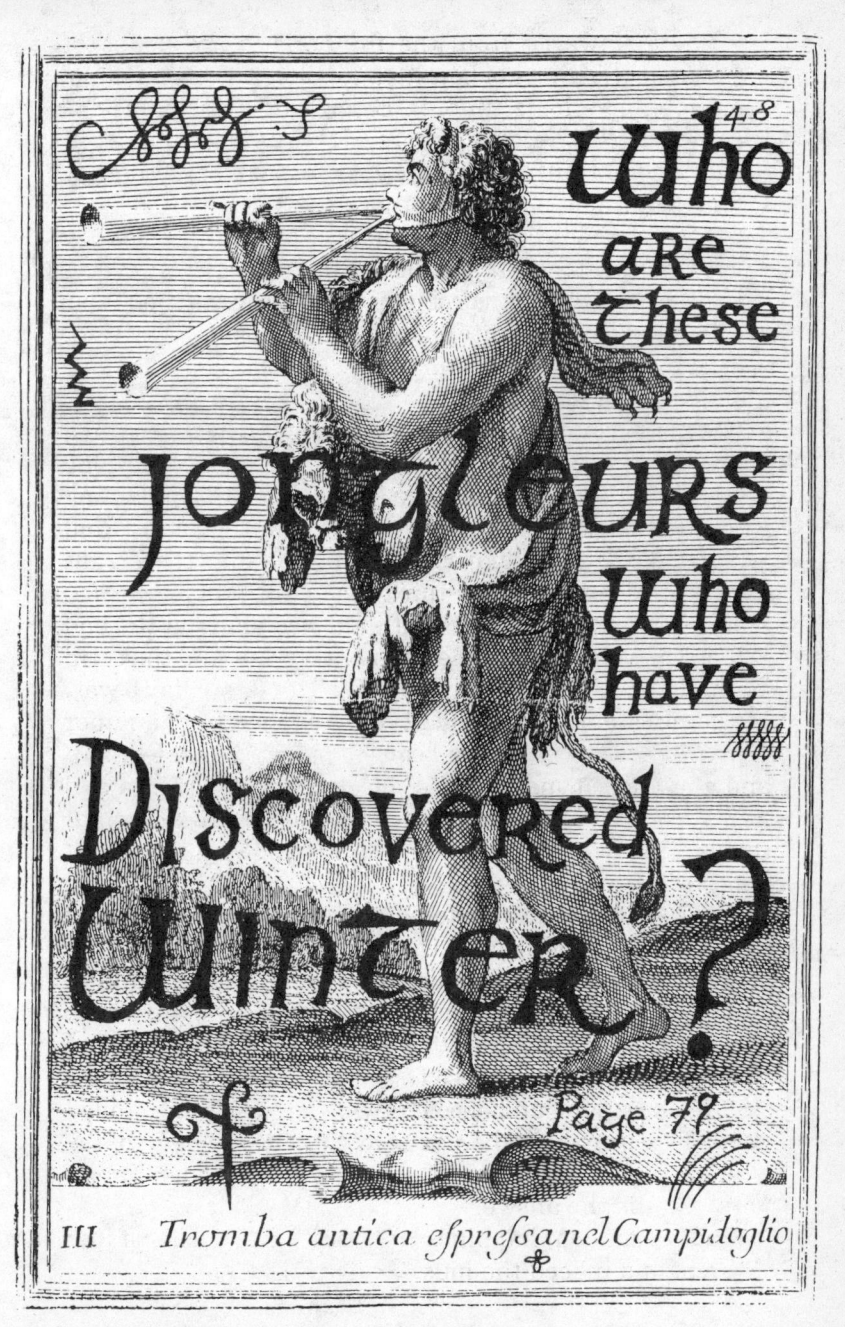

Who are these jongleurs who have Discovered Winter?

Page 79

III *Tromba antica espressa nel Campidoglio*

By the Sixteenth Century, the major ending had become so widespread that it had a proper name, the *Tierce de Picardie*, after the cathedral in Picardie that first championed its use. But its common name remained A Sudden Happiness because it described aptly the change from minor to major.

It was found that a piece of music, minor, having lived its life in misery but never having doubted that there was some point to it all, on being given the last rites in a major key to which it was not accustomed, looked back on its minor life and considered that it was not so bad after all. "The lowly shall be exalted!" they cried, and then died peacefully, holding the raised third to their breast.

The process of altering the third itself (pioneered by the monks of the early Church absolving the Wolf Fifth and the note B; their work carried on by the Frenchwoman) was called *musica ficta*, falseness in music, because it was the triumph of art over nature and science over nature, music over wind, poets over life.

But although *musica ficta* was indeed a good thing for the progress of music, it was not so felicitous for the young woman who had discovered A Sudden Happiness. In the process of her experiments she had absorbed so many of the discarded minor thirds through her skin that the level of despair in her body reached saturation point, and she developed a galloping cancer. She died before she had a chance to hear the fruits of her labours ringing out from *La Cathedrale de Notre Dame*. After the phosphorescence of her life then, came sudden and ironic sadness.

(Particles of Dust: the fourth adventure of the jongleurs)

In a suburb of South Auckland jongleurs have taken up with a group of women and have joined in their middle-of-the-morning coffee parties. They discover that this is an underworld lived upon the surface of the Earth. It is day but the women are dressed for evening, in elaborate nightgowns embroidered with tears, quilted dressing-gowns like animated bedspreads, and slippers edged with six-month-old kittens curled up to sleep. Thus got up (they have just got up) the women flit over the back fences between sections and congregate at the kitchen table of one of their number where they drink after-dinner coffee, though it is barely after breakfast.

The group of jongleurs who have wandered into this patch of darkness are welcomed with enthusiasm by the women.

"Oh, do come in!" exclaim the women, their faces filling the space of a back door. "The jug's just on."

Jongleurs have arrived uncomfortably in the boughs of a revolving clothesline, but manage to extricate their china bodies without injury, apart from chips in their outer garments.

"Phew!" they cry. "What a close one!"

They are invited immediately to join the book club, which needs members, but jongleurs decline saying they have a book of their own, a novelette, and they are only up to page seventy-two and they are not going to let themselves read another book until this one is finished. However, coffee mornings are just what jongleurs desire, and they take off their coats and hats to reveal more eveningish clothes, less tattered into the bargain, underneath.

A patch of night sky is seen stepping over a low fence in broad daylight by a passing postie. When he looks back — this because he could not believe his eyes the first time — he sees nothing and he prefers to believe in this absence as he continues with his round.

The women and the jongleurs, in the meantime, have arranged themselves in a circle alternating one with the other — woman, jongleur, woman, jongleur, like the segments of a roulette wheel — and they engage in a game of Chinese Whispers, also known as a round like a postal territory or a *rondeau* from the Middle Ages, and the epithet goes: "*Send more recruits in, we're going to advance*".

Jongleurs play their sackbuts as delicately as possible into the ears of the women, who pass on the snippets of information to the next person, a jongleur, their speech having the tenor of a reciting tone (although they are all sopranos and therefore well equipped to play the lead roles of men playing women in the operas of the Seventeenth Century). Jongleurs in their turn, receiving this music from the lips of the women, convert it once again into the speech of their instruments. The result is chance music, an improvisation of no fixed abode, wandering like minstrels, minnesingers, troubadours and trouvères, like the jongleurs themselves about the crooked roads and continents of a kitchen table. And for a time the kitchen is filled with the dense and intricate sound of many voices making a staggered pattern. The faces of the women shine. They laugh catching their breath between repetitions of, *"Send more recruits in, we're going to advance"*.

(And at that moment the postie reports to the dour troubadour that he has seen several jongleurs fitting the description stepping over a fence in South Auckland, and collects a substantial reward for his pains.)

A round is a circle, but it runs out. In this world there is no such thing as perfection. Where perfection occurs, as in the perfect interval of the fifth, it must be altered before it can be palatable to the human condition, just as the human condition must be tempered to avoid disappointment.

The human condition, when the round has finally come to its end (*"Send four and threepence, we're going to a dance"*), is a brief goodbye from the women, who announce suddenly that they must get on, they have things to do, and jongleurs find themselves alone in separate houses in the middle of suburbs. It has been so long they have forgotten what it is like to be so alone. Not seventeen jongleurs alone in one house, but seventeen jongleurs alone in seventeen houses. Their point of view is immediately reduced to one, what it was in the days before the woman, before the china factory and mass production.

"How did this happen!" they wail individually, with a variety of mountainous inflections.

Via a party of alarmed telephone conversations with the women recently returned to the daylight, jongleurs hear that there is no need to worry, this is merely the morning after and it is best passed in housewifely tasks.

Which is exactly what jongleurs do, all in their separate living rooms and kitchenettes, dusting the surfaces until they can see themselves in them (a small comfort), polishing the china figurines, ironing the sleeves, washing the plates and caressing the shapes of their fine bones. But none of this is at all to their taste. Instead of attending to the appearance of china ornaments, jongleurs would rather strike poses on the shadowbox themselves. Are they not after all china princes? They would rather stand gazing out into the room, their back to mirrored glass into which is absorbed everything. But here they are, china princes, jongleurs, tending these things.

If this is a dream, china princes would rather wake up.

If it is a novelette, they would rather write it than live it, is their opinion, or so they establish later when they compare notes.

In the early evening, assuming a casualness when dusting pianos — this air of indifference directed at the husbands and children just returned from the day — jongleurs, in collusion with each other but each in their separate suburban homes, strike a handful of notes, elopements, hoping the escape mechanisms on the pianos will work.

They do. How cold it is!

(The sameness of fictions)

There is still no word from his soul
although his body as always
is in attendance.
She once reeled a pillow
into a carriage and typed
parentheses there, hoping with these
to contain him in her bed
together with a dullness
the sheen on a fur cup once seen
in a museum. And he is still

in this bed but he is not in this
bed. What he has imagined
and what he has done —
is there any difference?

(Organum)

The practice of organum, two or more voices singing in parallel intervals of the perfect fourth, fifth and perfect octave, occurred spontaneously like the habit children adopt at a certain age, waist-high, of following their older siblings about.

Children, in their innocence, are models for the way the world is. A classful of infants who have not yet learned to hear music as they can taste sweetness, smell McDonald's outlets, and see a play area from a great distance (these senses developing in inverse proportions), being coaxed nevertheless to sing in unison, will some of them take a note at the interval of a fifth below that of the rest of the class. Entire nursery rhymes are sung in this manner. And although these wayward children are encouraged to lip-sync by a teacher who would like all to sing as one (there are many points of view but there is only one view), and who mouths insults at them, her back turned to an audience of parents, there is a certain perfection in their choice of harmony. The perfection is that of the perfect fifth, the dividing of strings, the exquisiteness of temperament, and the devil-may-care of how tonality came into existence.

Not to be outdone by these *enfants terribles*, the men and women of the Ninth and Tenth centuries, singing plainsong melodies to the glory of God, took up with organum and they took to organum. They sang in perfect fourths, fifths and at octaves with each other, according to their gender, their temperament, and the colour of their hair.

Blonde women sang soprano, brunettes alto, and women whose hair could variously be described as driftwood, hazel, chestnut, second debut, were blessed with the voice of a mezzo-soprano. In the same way the men were divided into tenors, basses and baritones (also an artisan class of barber, but that is another story).

Occasionally a singer with an eye for the main chance, perhaps vying for a place in the cathedral choir at Mainz, would try to get away with adopting another voice, one that they knew was required, more often than not a higher one. And that was how the dyeing of hair came into use. There were often, however, the telltale roots of chords and the straining for these notes where they appeared at the top of the register. It was often said of a woman with the blondest hair but her head notes so obviously foundering, "Oh she's just a bottle blonde!" There was also the practice of the counter-tenor, castrated at twelve, cast forever in the loveliness of his boyhood, dyeing his boy-soprano blond hair the darker, more honeyed, sapiential blonde of a woman. But generally men and men and women and women, all in their vocal registers, got along quite amicably leading their lives a perfect fifth apart.

(Organum)

A phenomenon discovered by Mr Hugh Tracey of the African Music Society, is that certain tribes in South Africa are still singing in consecutive fifths — this according to the *Oxford Companion*. The reader of the *Oxford Companion* is perhaps regarding Mr Tracey as Mr Tracey is regarding the tribes of South Africa.

(The Gift of Tears Rent in Garments: the fifth adventure of the jongleurs)

In their time they have all gone to fancy-dress parties dressed as the woman in the streetmap, wearing an assortment of skirts, blouses and cardigans, and paying particular attention to a version of face and a matching in the matter of shoes and handbags.

At a masked ball disguised as a blessing, they stand out like sore thumbs, nuns among a crowd of religious sisters, monks, clowns, angels, nymphs and shepherds hired from the local thespian society. They are used to the startling prominence they have in the convent along with all the other uniformly dressed Sisters of Mercy who nevertheless are unique in the eyes of God. Here, they have nothing to do with their hands although their souls are, as always, well occupied. Despite the dispensing of small mercies among the small talk of the party, the controlling of their moods, the tides and also the weather, together with the vagaries of their dress — the nuns at this party are not a success. As it turns out, their early departure is a blessing in disguise, because they must be up by 2 a.m. for the singing of Matins.

In the early hours they sing Gregorian Chant that over the centuries has stretched into a melisma, a sequence, that is the singing of many notes to one syllable of the text. A stave first drawn in the Seventh Century has become a motorway of many lanes. *Kyrie eleison* can take twenty minutes to get to the end of as the syllables try every possible route in their search for an exit from this world — but to no avail. The chapel abounds with echoes, notes returning from the marble walls and the soffits on the ceiling. The nuns, each shrouded in a veil, feel compassion for these poor thwarted souls and see that, despite their carryings-on, they are nevertheless very beautiful, the sound of them. And everything shall be given for this beauty, even happiness. And they take them in and bring them up as their own; and they are — their own.

Jongleurs are wandering about the convent garden in the early hours of the morning after a night at a masked ball. To their astonishment they have been let in the convent gate. The Church has apparently revised its thinking on itinerant musicians, Common Time, and profane songs. "We knew all along they'd come round," say the jongleurs. They have on their gold-dipped frills and flounces. They attended the ball as a band of jongleurs, thinking it a good joke to go as their ordinary selves. They spent the evening entertaining the other guests with the contents of the *chansonnier* which is rapidly acquiring a following (including the dour troubadour who makes hasty journeys but never quite gets there). Now they are entertained by the women, their melisma in the distance as they sing Lauds, which is intoned at dawn. How nice it is to be together again, muse the jongleurs, and in such meditative surroundings. The pink dawn throws its colour into the sky. The garden is slower to give up its shadows. In the half-light jongleurs discover a tree trained to grow in symmetrical strands against a warm wall. As it is nearing the end of winter, the tree is covered in buds. Jongleurs freeze momentarily when they see this, a tree with small buds, a threat to their very nature, what they are made of and therefore what is the matter with them.

"What of winter, winter, winter and winter?" wails one jongleur as if referring to a firm of lawyers.

To keep calm, jongleurs put their hands in their Chinese sleeves where there are a few stray leaves gathered once in a domain, and they remind themselves that an exhibition of warmth is after all what they have always wanted, that the approach of spring is nothing to be alarmed about.

The nuns, emerging from the chapel, a multiplicity of person pulling notes tenderly along on trainer wheels behind, have found to their delight that many hands make light bulbs. They tell the jongleurs that they are looking forward to the spring, with its sudden profusion of daffodils, jonquils, irises and freesias.

"Come," they beckon the jongleurs, keeping their voices low, "come and entertain the Abbess. She is confined to her cell but receives visitors."

Jongleurs can't believe the change in Church doctrine that allows them in, but they follow the perambulating nuns through the soft grounds to the monastery, where the women have occupied a wing, and occupied it thoroughly, their habits draped everywhere, from cellar to belfry, there are so many of them.

"The fame of our Abbess has spread far and wide," whispers a young nun as they all enter the cloister.

Soon jongleurs are ushered into a small cell where the walls drip as if with tears. It is occupied by a very wan nun reclining on a hard narrow bed with no more than a swatch for a pillow, a length of flannel for a blanket. Jongleurs are urged to be silent by nuns holding fingers cruciform with their lips. This is the Abbess. She is caught in the most reckless pose, her head thrown back, one arm held aloft, body arched, and as for her face — her eyes heavy-lidded, her lips ajar in an expression of ecstasy. She appears to be transfixed by the ceiling, and a stream of fetishes issues from her mouth.

Two monks at her bedside scribble furiously, one deciphers the scrambled language, the other illuminates, more slowly, these same phrases.

Before long, as if grown accustomed to the dark, jongleurs find they can understand the words. This is what they hear:

"I see a woman clad entirely in gold leaf. I know this woman instantly to be Sapientia, the Knowledge of God, though I have never before laid eyes on her. Now there is the Virgin wearing the raiment of the sun, and weeping. She says, 'I am weeping over the iniquity of the world!' Angels are dancing in the precipitation. Now there is another woman, tattered and distraught, pulled this way and that among clouds. 'Where are you going?' I cannot but ask her. She does not reply. I see a band of men dressed in a profusion of china hats and coats, vests, ties and sleeves, against the extreme cold. They look to be engaged in the making of music, professionally, not the music of the Heavens, but of the Earths. They carry a *chansonnier*, and the wind riffles through their vocal cords. The wind was not there until the vocal cords stopped it in its tracks."

The Abbess catches her breath and sits up suddenly, snapping her eyes wide awake, casting her blanket from her shoulders. She fixes the jongleurs with a searching stare. "Hail! Who are you and what is your business?"

The jongleurs, flushed with delight at being addressed by the Abbess, reply, "We are jongleurs — well, that is our chosen profession anyhow. Often we just go as plain china princes," they finish modestly.

"And I am Hildegard of Bingen," says the Abbess. "I am not yet of Bingen, but one day I will be, you mark my words."

Jongleurs nod nervous agreement, then Hildegard says, "You could give us a tune, jongleurs."

Which they do.

Hildegard lies back and listens, swinging her ankle, and when the *chanson* of romantic love is finished, she remarks, "Your music is very ornate — and you have discovered winter, no?"

"Oh yes, Saint!" clamour the jongleurs. "There is winter, winter, winter and winter!"

"Jongleurs," says Hildegard, "it need not *always* be winter."

When jongleurs look blank, Hildegard sighs and says, "Never mind." Then she adds, "We have had a troubadour at the monastery asking after you. But no matter, he can cool his heels while you entertain us."

It is obvious the Abbess is quite taken with her little band of jongleurs. She leans from her couch and fingers their clothes. "My dears, look, your sleeves are tattered from the rigours of lives lived in faith." And she turns to the scribe and says, "They have received the Gift of Tears Rent in Garments, for they have given up worldly goods."

The other monk meanwhile illuminates the steady chink of tears as they fall.

"There are many of you," observes Hildegard presently.

"Yes," reply the jongleurs in unison. "We want to see everything from all angles."

"Oh? Is that so?" says Hildegard.

Jongleurs shuffle shyly.

"It wasn't, by any chance, love?"

Jongleurs clear their throats. "Love?"

"That you became plural to escape the claustrophobic feelings of love? Is that it, hmm?"

"No no," reply the jongleurs. "We have never even been in love. Like you, Saint, we are individuals."

Then one of them, in a burst, adds, "We were once in a dream."

"Ah, a dream!" says Hildegard. The scribe and the artist immediately take up their pens, but Hildegard motions them at-ease.

"Yes, a dream," continues the confessional jongleur. "But you see, Saint, it was very ordinary."

"Ordinary to the point of tedium," chips in another.

"To the point of tedium," chants the first. "It was not quite our dream."

"It was someone else's dream?" asks Hildegard.

"Perhaps," says the jongleur elusively. "And then we saw . . ."

"Yes?" ask Hildegard, the scribe, the artist, and all the company of postulants.

"That we could leave the dream."

"Ah!"

"That we could have a few adventures of our own, that's all, better than the dreams, but not enough to distract us from writing the novelette. And we did, leave that is."

Hildegard sighs. "So you're writing a novelette?"

"Oh yes," say the jongleurs altogether. "It is nine years old!"

"We are writing it and also we are living it," says the confessional jongleur.

"Oh my dear jongleurs!" says Hildegard, chuckling to herself, but not unkindly. "Do you not know? It is not necessary to live it! Oh my goodness me! Oh my petit jongleurs! Imagine if I had to live all the things that happen on my ceiling!"

And she and the monks put their heads together and laugh merrily.

Jongleurs look askance. They catch each other's eyes, frowns furrowing their brows. By unspoken consensus they agree it is time to leave the Saint, and they shuffle their china bodies towards the door.

Hildegard hastens, "Oh jongleurs, don't leave! Just think on my words. Stay and delight us with your sad music that has such happy endings."

And so jongleurs once more put their sackbuts to their lips and a music, a wind, it is difficult to tell which, riffled through the instruments and wound its way along the corridors and issued finally through the grille in the wall.

(And the dour troubadour, roaming distractedly in the monastery garden, hears a tune, barely recognisable, from his budget of songs, and this is the first time he has heard the famous embellishment. And although he jumps up and down in anger and in frustration at not being let into the allegorist's cell, he can not but notice the sound is divine, wondrous, inspired by God.)

(An article of her faith)

She believes she is entertaining him. He has no thought for entertaining her, but all the same, she imagines he does, and thus entertains herself.

(Florid Organum: an allegory illustrating the allegory)

There was once a monk but despite this he was not a happy man. He had joined the monastery for the love of a woman who, sadly, did not love him. In her defence, lest she be thought cold-hearted, it is fair to say she did not know of his existence.

We will call him the Anonymous Monk of Santiago de Compostella, because that was his name. Now, the Anonymous Monk of Santiago de Compostella had always thought there was the whole world and then there was this woman, and that it was to be one or the other, never both together. On the day he finally came to his senses, touched them, and realised it was not going to be the other, never would be, he entered the monastery where he believed the rest of the world, apart from the woman, was contained, if only one knew precisely where to look, or to listen. Notwithstanding this enlightenment, occurring like a day between the darkness of the cloister and the darkness of death, he was not very happy. He would rather have had the woman and the shadow she cast over all the world, eclipsing it, than all the enlightenment to be had in Christendom.

The woman was quite an extraordinary man. She was, in reality, a woman, but she thought like a man and she spoke like a man. This despite the fact she had lived in a community of women for the past several years, and before that had led an increasingly solitary existence, following her life back from the time we are speaking of. At eighteen she took the Benedictine habit, as was the habit of Benedictine men. In her middle teens she learned Latin and music, like men, the difference being that all the while she was the recipient of feminine visions she dared not tell anyone about. In her early teens, under pressure to conform, she learned embroidery, tapestry and the wiles of illness. In her childhood she gained enlightenment. At eight she was given to the Church, walled up with a woman, her tutor. At three she saw her first vision, and at birth she became the tenth child of ten, the tithe, the blessing with which to bless.

It was when she was twelve that the Anonymous Monk of Santiago de Compostella, himself still a mere child, first caught sight of her. He happened to be passing the monastery at Mount St Disibod on an errand when he saw, peering out through a grille in the wall, the most beautiful face he had ever laid eyes on. It was the face of a young girl looking up at a skyful of birds. This was all he ever knew of her — her face chequered by small iron bars and the transparent measures of her tears, but he fell instantly in love with this face; there was nothing he would not have done for the love of this face.

Much of his early youth was spent keeping a lonely vigil outside the walls of the monastery, hoping for a glimpse of the chequered girl. Also hoping that one day she would be released from her schooling and would walk demurely, wearing a long cloak, through the gates of the monastery, her eyes wide after her years of confinement. And the first person (I) she would lay eyes on in the small world that exists outside the cloister would be the Anonymous Monk of Santiago de Compostella. And the Anonymous Monk of

Santiago de Compostella would sweep her into his arms — this is how he imagined it, knowing that in reality he would, if he could find the courage, stoop to one knee and ask timidly for her hand in marriage.

At the age of fourteen he noticed two things. The first was that every time the girl appeared, as on the first occasion, flocks of starlings formed themselves into hearts and rosaries in the sky above the monastery. The second was that there was a pattern to the young postulant's appearances. They occurred on Sundays and the holy days of the Church. When he was sure these events were no coincidence, he began to wonder if the beautiful face was not a vision and he himself the recipient of the grace of God through the intercession of the Virgin appearing before him. He could not imagine how such beauty could have compiled itself into one mortal face. Therefore the latter part of his youth was spent contemplating one of the great mysteries of the Church: whether his eyes deceived him.

He busied himself otherwise, bridging the gap between this world and the next, by writing love poems of which the following is an example, showing his liberal borrowings and lendings:

Hail, thou, full of the grace of birds and the holy aura of your face. Blessed art though among the inmates of monasteries, and wretched are the bars that thee imprison!

Then one day (he remembers it as the blackest day of his life) he saw the astonishing visage appear at the grille and look up at the sky, as was her wont. But on this day her head was shrouded in a great darkness. She had taken the veil.

The Anonymous Monk of Santiago de Compostella, now aged eighteen and the age of despair, immediately left the vicinity of St Disibod's and sought a monastery as far away as possible. He came to rest at the monastery of Santiago de Compostella in north-west Spain. And the Anonymous Monk of Santiago de Compostella had finally reached Santiago de Compostella.

After seven years he took the sleeves of the patron, Iago el Mayor, and began the life of a fully professed religious. However, as he suffered from asthma, he was relieved from heavy duties about the monastery, the gathering of apples, the kneading of dough, and the contemplation of mysteries. Instead he took to drink, and he took to drink like a duck to water. He took holy orders and he took drink. And he drank sack and sack was his most preferred drink.

Then it happened that the musical director of the monastery, a very musical man and a very direct man, famed for his choirs, died. And the Anonymous Monk of Santiago de Compostella was put in charge of music, which was considered a light duty because of the weightlessness of notes. Amd now there was much notating and singing and listening to fill his days and his nights, and also the early hours of the morning. But now he pined away in the choir loft rather than in his cell, thinking of nothing but the girl he had wanted to marry. He could not rid himself of the image of her face, which lived in his head as if she had the lease there. Sometimes the telephone rang and it was always for her.

His own face, due to an abundance of sack, took on the texture of roses and trellises. The shadows of the bars dividing the holy face of the girl matted his cheeks.

With his mind occupied by the woman who lived in it, the singing of plainsong, which should have been his primary concern, came a very poor second. The part of the Mass under his jurisdiction (the Ordinary of the Mass, which changed every day; the Proper could look after itself) was sung in unison or in perfect fifths, according to the custom of the day which took into account the various shades of the hair of the men. But the Anonymous Monk of Santiago de Compostella, his mind on other things such as a woman reclining on a couch on the right side of his brain, and his brain befuddled by quantities of sack, found increasingly (moving forwards through his life, as was his wont) that he could not find the note it was intended he should sing. He would have several tries, stabbing at notes all around the intended. The other monks, being of sympathetic natures, would wait on the prescribed note until the lovestruck monk at last arrived at it. Then they would all proceed together to the next note, only to have the same thing happen. In this way was plainsong ornamented.

Now it happened that a twelve-year-old musical prodigy was visiting Santiago de Compostella along with his father. He was brought to the monastery especially to hear the monks sing, because talk of the abilities of the previous musical director had spread far and wide and he was a very far-flung little boy. As he installed himself with his father in the front pew of the chapel, there was great consternation going on behind the scenes. Attempts to keep the Anonymous Monk sober had, of course, failed. The Abbot, and indeed all the monks, were well aware they were not going to impress this boy genius as they would have done in the days of the old musical director. However, they could not but go on, and this they did, with the whispered encouragement that music was for the glory of God and God, come hell or high water, would be glorified.

As the monks began, in their inimitable manner, a rendering of the Introit that had been the staple of Church music for the past three hundred years, the boy and his father settled back to hear once again what they had heard many times before. The boy prided himself on knowing every note of it. It was therefore a mere matter of seconds before he realised something was very awry with one of the voices. And he listened and he heard and he saw the bombardment of many extra notes against the ceiling of the chapel. And these notes returned to him as splendour, and he thought, This is indeed the music of God! And he took out his theory book and began scribbling down the embellished organum as fast as the monks could sing it.

At the end of the Introit the Anonymous Monk of Santiago de Compostella peered groggily over the railings, expecting to be berated by the twelve-year-old prodigy. But the boy stood on his seat and applauded, shouting, "Bravo! Bravo! Bravissimo!" and turned his back on the Blessed Sacrament because it was from the monks, he believed, came the true divinity.

The boy and his father took the manuscript of the Introit to Rome to show it to the Pope of the day, who was Pope Hildebrand, Gregory VII, and the Pope had the Vatican choir sing the Introit and when they had finished he asked the boy, "From whence came such godliness?" The boy could only say that it came from an anonymous monk of Santiago de Compostella, with a florid complexion. And from then on, as the music was dispensed all through the monasteries and cathedrals of the Holy Roman Empire, the ornamenting of God was called Florid Organum.

The woman whose face was so beloved by the Anonymous Monk of Santiago de Compostella was now Abbess of the convent attached to the monastery of St Disibod. On hearing Florid Organum for the first time she clasped her hands to her breast, thanked God for such beauty, and Florid Organum moved bodily into the right side of her brain.

As for the Anonymous Monk, when the Pope sent word to Santiago de Compostella to the effect that he would like to decorate further his already florid complexion, all the monk could say was, How he still loved that face!

(After Breugel: *The Allegory of Hearing*)

A flock of monks
descended from a dove
divine inspiration
who once suggested
texts, melodies in waiting
of the liturgy
plainsong like plain
scones, no embellishment (such
as a bunch of grapes or
quavers boiled for jelly)
nothing will cloud
their passage into this world
via the ear of the
Pope of the day
and of the Dark Ages

Gregory the fallen from a Great
Height was his title
also Pope Gregory I am
I am and a first-year course
in the Ides of a long
march from Rome to Avignon
also St Cloud Upon Which
I Will Build My Church
and he has received
a music, the wind, all moods
for the glory of God
that is the theory and Magic
Realist is also his name
but actually these notes
their nomenclature
are the realest moments
of his entire life.

IV

An Exhibition of the Warmth of a Man and a Woman Growing Against a Warm Wall

(After William of Conches: a forecast)

The warmest woman
is colder than the
coldest man.

(An audience with the Pope, almost)

And the Pope, who was Pope Eugenius III, sent an emissary to Hildegard to inquire after these visions, their shape and size and the texture of them and the frequency of them, and their pitch; and the emissary, upon entering the cell and seeing condensation running down the walls, said, "It is hot in here"; whereupon Hildegard replied, "It is cold." And this was reported back to Pope Eugenius and Pope Eugenius considered it, wiping his brow (it was July), and said, "Hildegard indeed has the gift."

(Angels clap their hands to keep warm)

They have returned to the Domain in which they first experienced the cold. They have come here for a reason, it wasn't just by chance, their usual mode of transport. They have come here to talk and in the middle of the Domain, they all put their heads together to do precisely that.

The matter has not been mentioned before, but jongleurs are growing very weary of their adventures. Although they have long been disciples of what they would like, they can see very well that the rigours of this life are taking their toll, that the disadvantages may outweigh the advantages. "Just look at our ragged garments!" they cry. Their beautiful sleeves now hanging in tatters.

"Oh!" they sigh.

It's not just the sleeves.

"The sleeves are a metaphor," says one jongleur and the others nod. They know that. Oh how they all did so want to live the novelette!

"Though we say it ourselves," they say, "the imaginary life is not, um, completely fulfilling."

They compare notes, pacing about among the classical statuary.

It's like this: once two or three monasteries have been visited, well, they are all more or less the same after that. It is the same with convents; they also are the same (although different). And with the suburbs. Before long, everything is the same, even the most astonishing thing that jongleurs have ever laid eyes on. It is no more astonishing than the last most astonishing thing. A fur cup in the early morning, for instance, is no longer a novelty.

But what choice do they have, jongleurs?

"Is there ever any choice in these matters!" asks a despairing jongleur rhetorically from a park bench.

"Oh, don't be such a wet blanket," says another. "We're all in this together."

But it's true. What choice do they have but to continue with their adventures? They know no other way. They know nothing, only wondering. One of them once said to the woman (in the days when they were single), "I know nothing!" — despising the fact that she knew everything (even though she protested she did not).

"Her realness began to fade from view," muses one jongleur.

"That was a long time ago," says another.

"A novelette is a possession," says yet another, a calmer jongleur, taking charge. "Agreed?"

"Agreed," snuffle the others.

"Okay, that's basic. And we can't live without possessions, right? If there was no such thing as an article of clothing, a musical instrument, a dancing bear, a piano

If you look in one place long enough you will see a woman

XXVI Serpentone

concerto, the memoirs of a saint, the movements of eyes, an angel, a vision or a poem — how would we know we were here and not there? Tell me that."

No one can find an answer.

Later, as they all sit soaking their feet in mirrors planted in a miniature garden among bridges and pavilions made of porcelain — this because of the exhaustion an adventure causes — a thought strikes jongleurs and that is: if the novelette were not this way, then their lives would not be this way either. So all it takes is to change the novelette. And they wonder why, with all their astronomical inventions, they did not think of this small simplicity before.

A shy jongleur, one who speaks rarely, not from want of trying, who opens and shuts his mouth often like a gaping fish, now clears his throat and raises his voice, "Um, excuse me. Excuse me!" A grudging silence. "Is it necessary to live it at all, the novelette that is...I mean, remember the Abbess — 'Oh my dear jongleurs!' " and he opens his palms tropically in one of the theatrical gestures that are sometimes the prerogative of the very timid.

Everyone listens politely but no one takes any notice, and when he has finished, the shy jongleur, the others turn their attention back to the first solution, that of the tenor of the novelette. And from this solution, held aloft in a test tube with the sun shining through it so that the atoms all the more cling to each other at the excitement of the approach of summer, comes another question and that is: Who has written the novelette? After all, there are seventeen china princes (jongleurs, say the jongleurs).

(Rapid eye movement)

And when word had travelled throughout Europe (reading a book in the street, its small eccentricity) of the nun Hildegard who had seen great things, the scholars and theologians of the Church made a deputation to St Disibod's to see her, this woman who had seen.

But now there occurred a dramatic irony. Hildegard, who was once witness to a great light, was now subject to a multitude of small lights shining out from the admiration of the scholars and theologians, and she found herself bathed in light, and therefore unable to take light. And although she looked up towards the ceiling in the pose that had come to be interpreted as one of ecstasy, she could see only darkness compared with the illumination of her own body.

And although she liked visions, had become accustomed to visions, had seen visions since the age of eight when she was walled up with nothing else but what she might like to see — nevertheless Hildegard found she also liked being bathed in the light emanating from the admiration of holy men, and she thought she could very easily become accustomed to that. And Hildegard discovered that to be seen is not to see; that being seen and seeing are opposites as light and dark are opposites; as wondering and knowing.

Still the scholars and theologians clustered about her, gazing up at what to them was darkness but it was their belief that for Hildegard the ceiling contained a great light. And they looked to Hildegard, in her struck pose, to spill the secrets of the ceiling from her lips.

And Hildegard found herself in a dilemma — the first dilemma of her life, her life at the monastery being sheltered from such things as what to wear, whether to confide, even whether to doubt. If she revealed to the scholars and theologians that she saw only what they did — a blackness, perhaps a crack like the crease in the palm of the hand — they might never believe her again, and she could spend the rest of her life as she did her first twenty years, in anonymity, in almost solitude.

She therefore proceeded to wonder, whereas before, the recipient of the undoubted gifts of the ceiling, she had known. And as she had known aloud, now she wondered aloud.

And the scholars and theologians continued to listen with rapt attention to the visions that clattered at her feet, and they believed every word.

"Oh Hildegard, Hildegard!" they cried. "Hildegard indeed has the Gift!"

But as soon as they had gone and she was alone in darkness, the mysteries of the ceiling were revealed to her.

(Fate befalling the shape and sound of a plate in a room)

It is after all the way
atoms have fallen, an

audience of angels dancing
attendance and a square

dance. The quiet life
of a dinnerplate wanting

for nothing but to make
the musics of God to the

glory of God and to take
sighing a mysterious vow

of the absence of sound
its vast presence. John

Cage said, A plate in a room
makes the sound of a plate

in a room (and the room
makes the sound of a winter

cabbage or thoughtfulness)
this until
crossing the room, a fall

and then it makes the sound
of the immense suffering of the world.

(*Modus operandi* or, after Vatican II, a mode of transport)

In a museum which they have entered to escape, momentarily, the cold (also to see warmth displayed in glass cases) is an auditorium for the performance of music, and jongleurs, this is very much to their liking. They have been used to making music out of doors where notes are free to go as far as the clouds before returning to Earth (or to leave this world if their escape art is successful). The idea of a concert chamber for the containing of notes intrigues the jongleurs. They study its acoustics, a map of the paths that notes will travel.

"Look, a Middle C whizzes round this curve in the wall faster than any of the other notes," cries an excited jongleur, "whereas a B-flat makes the light fittings reverberate!"

Jongleurs consider the possibility that their chance music, the passing of cars on a motorway, a composition they discovered once in the slow movement of a rush hour, might make an interesting program for a concert.

However, when they inquire about installing their instruments they are told by a uniformed custodian that there is no room in the auditorium for a motorway.

"But what about that?" they object, pointing to the concert pit which appears to be running smoothly.

"The placing of a subway station at the submerged podium is not without difficulty," replies the curator stiffly.

"Oh the difficulty of everything!" cry several china jongleurs at once.

"Yeah, well," says the curator. "The two forty-five from Notre Dame is already two minutes late," he adds consulting his watch.

Undaunted, jongleurs sit on the steps of the concert pit and hastily arrange their composition for a consort of sackbuts instead of the cars. There is a great flurry of manuscript paper, the hoarse whisper of pencils, and the soft bodies of rubbers rolling onto the floor. In no time they have set the theme tune (which is nothing you could whistle) for sackbuts. It is *musique concrète* — music built from blocks of natural sound which then become something more perfect and more permanent than nature. They entitle it, after a small conference, *A Wind in the Aeolian Mode Trapped by a Tree in the Twelfth Century* and mark it at the top *to be played with feeling*, although as jongleurs know well, there was no such thing in the Middle Ages.

The composition completed, they hand it to the curator, who says, "Ta very much," without thinking what he is saying.

(Clouds, clouds, a soffit among them)

She was always lost but now she has lost lost. Even a streetmap would be of no earthly use because she has found herself in the intervals between streets, also between the branches of trees, between notes, and in the dark recesses between stars. She is pulled this way and that, her clothes are torn by sudden suction and hang raggedly. Once she said she believed her life was conducted according to rhyme, but there is no rhyme or reason to these movements.

"Oh my dear rained upon!" she murmurs.

She is quite lost.

One twilight, or dawn, it being always halfway between night and day, the woman looks down from a place shared with angels, notes eloping, dead souls, shooting stars, the occasional overdue orienteer, and happens to see something she thinks she recognises as slightly familiar. She feels a small excited gasp escape her lips, because this is the first hint of anything familiar she has seen in living memory. It was in fact a faint music that attracted her attention; in the distance, subliminal almost, like the unheard music of Whole Health centres. This melody — you could hardly call it that, a string of notes, a mystery — cause her to look down. This is what she sees:

A community of monks, their hands elusive in their sleeves, are singing plainsong, after Pope Gregory, according to the grapes that fall from their beards onto the page.

A coven of nuns, all looking the same in their chaste habits but busy sewing the most outlandish plainclothes (being careful not to jab the angels partying about the sparks at the ends of the pins), are minding a class of little gracenotes while they work. And in the monastery garden against the warmest wall to be found in winter, a man and a woman, espalier, entwined, are growing together.

Although one would expect this to be the subject of much astonishment for the woman watching from above, it is the littlest bit old hat. For instance, the knowledge of how careful one must be with pins is not at all new to her (and Sapientia was dressed entirely in gold leaf). And the fusion of the couple is not in the least surprising.

After a while the woman notices a troupe of jongleurs singing and dancing and playing upon sackbuts for the entertainment of anyone who cares to listen. And the woman listens and, peering closer, gives another little start, "Oh!" as she recognises the sackbuts as those fallen from a tree that flowered once outside her bedroom window. The jongleurs she recognises from their china bodies as replicas of the very same china prince who left her early one morning before she had woken. She saw them leave in her dream; her dream watched them go and then her dream also departed. She followed.

"Well, what else was I supposed to do?" she asks.

Presently the jongleurs, still dressed in the Chinese sleeves she ironed carefully the night before the fatal morning, now ragged, and in the tattered remnants of her own body, put aside their singing and dancing, sit down in a circle with their sackbuts and an audience of allcomers, monks and nuns and women in elaborate dressing-gowns, etc., and they begin to read from a large thumbed notebook. And the words come from a wind riffling through their vocal chords.

Straining to hear above the traffic of notes, comets and departing souls around her, the woman hears a jongleur begin a story.

"This is *Musica Ficta*," he says, and stops. "And this is what it's about." He clears his throat. "A young boy becomes a prince, for obvious reasons. The prince becomes a vagabond — it's stifling being a rich kid. The vagabond becomes a jongleur because that is the fashion, and it becomes his greatest ambition that he should live between one note and another, like Mozart. But then the jongleur meets a woman."

Here he pauses.

"And?" coax the audience. They are sprawled on the grass, drinking from cardboard casks of wine.

"And?" says the woman to herself. She realises, not with a sense of deja vu but with the certainty of it, that the history the jongleurs are telling is the life she herself has imagined. She could well continue.

"And?" repeat the audience.

The story goes on, illustrated with frequent bursts on sackbuts. Another jongleur takes it up. "And so the newly in-love jongleur became china — well, everything was so delicate, no? Collapsible. And he had this job in a china factory because there was no money in jongling, so there were the means, right in front of him, and then —"

He pauses again, the audience leans closer. Notes from sackbuts bounce off the clouds lining the sky, right next to the woman, and they return to the audience as the sound of thunder and everyone is thoroughly amazed.

"And *then*," continues the china prince, "the china prince became many, times, multiples — see?" He takes a bow. "Take a bow," he says to the assembled princes, jongleurs, whatever. They all take a bow. "And this was in order to see everything from as many angles as possible. You never know what you might miss. There is only one view, but there are many points of view."

"It wasn't *quite* like that," says the woman in a low voice.

And at the same moment that the *Ficta* and the life the woman has imagined become one, as the fitting together of atoms into molecules, the voices of the jongleurs stop and are replaced by a flight of polite clapping, and an atom turns over in its sleep, shunting the one next to it, and the one next to that, and so on. And there is the minutest thrill among everything in the universe.

(A man and a woman entertained by the weather)

They have stolen each other's thunder. What is written in the *Ficta* is what she has imagined, and what she has imagined, she has read in the *Ficta*. But who has written the *Ficta*?

(The anonymous monk takes the name of his father, and of his son, and of the author of the manuscript: after *A History of Western Music*)

There was once a monk who protected his identity by going under his own name. This was the cleverest of disguises. He was a composer of motets and of Masses, but more so of secular songs and dances. He wrote *rondeaux* and *virelais*, using several voices at once, polyphony, which was considered very Ars Nova, the avant garde of the Fourteenth Century. This is not to say he was not given to the more traditional customs such as three beats per measure, but given also to the pleasures of the flesh, being of large mass and the father of numerous illegitimate children. He was also a poet and he took the name of a poet, his own, and once he wrote *My end is my beginning and my beginning my end*. Having taken holy orders his art came from the society of sameness where difference flourishes.

Now at that time, in all musics, whether sacred or profane, the composer remained anonymous. It was as if these musics came from the same voice, an oeuvre incorporating the whole of Christendom in its plethora of styles and signatures, a large voice like the voice of God. But in the midst of this voice the anonymous monk wrote a Mass, and because this Mass was out of the Ordinary compared with the other masses that were its contemporaries, it attracted much attention, and the anonymous monk attracted more attention than would normally have been given a mere composer. The Mass itself had a name, according to custom — how they would be able to tell musics apart if both the composer *and* the composition were nameless? — and that name was *La Messe de Notre*

Dame. And presently people hearing its four voices began to wonder whose was the fifth, the silent voice — who had written this *Messe de Notre Dame*? Who could have conceived of such difference?

There was the Ordinary of the Mass and the Proper of the Mass, and in the Twelfth and Thirteenth centuries composers had been primarily interested in setting the Proper; the *Gradual,* the *Alleluia*, etc., whose texts changed every day according to the change in the liturgical season. And the parts of the Mass had fallen together by accident, a catastrophe in the universe — an *Alleluia* by one composer, an *Introit* by another, and a *Tract* by yet another — with no account taken as to whether one mode sounded well following another. Or whether one composer's idiosyncratic motifs, as in individuals peppering their speech with particular repeated phrases, clashed with that of the next. For was it not true that all musics were of one voice, and all composers were of one voice, and that voice was the voice of God, divine inspiration transported by a dove?

In the Fourteenth Century the Ars Nova movement, which included the particular anonymous monk we are concerned with, saw changes not of season but the slow change of climate. The *Messe* of the anonymous monk would have defied description a century before but as we are travelling forwards in time we can easily describe it. It was a setting not just of the Proper, as had been the rule, but of the Ordinary as well; a setting for four voices, one of them, the counter-tenor, perhaps being performed by an instrument rather than a human voice. The Ordinary of the Mass contained the *Kyrie, Gloria, Credo, Sanctus, Agnus Dei* and the *Ite, missa est* ("Go, you are dismissed"): the parts of the Mass that do not change, are constant — it is always winter. Within this winter the anonymous monk interlocked voices to keep out the cold. He sorted motifs and he matched modes, like shoes and handbags, so one section of the Mass would sound pleasing following on from another.

And because *La Messe de Notre Dame* was so different, people were curious and asked, "Who has written this Mass?"

The answer was, "An anonymous monk has written it."

And the next question was, "Who is the anonymous monk?"

The answer was, "Guillaume," because that was his name.

The next question was, "And where does he come from?"

And the answer to that was, "Machaut," because that was the place of his birth.

When all this was known there was no more wondering about the authorship of *La Messe de Notre Dame*, it was Guillaume de Machaut, and Guillaume de Machaut became a household name. And in due course there was no more wondering about the identity of subsequent creative anonymous monks.

But in distinguishing between one composer and another there appeared quite suddenly — like a wind sprung up between pressure fronts — a school of sleeves hissing singly across pages, the private sighing of inspired voices, and the vibrating of ears whispered into by flocks of doves in the very early morning. And composers discovered that with authorship must come anonymity, just as there must be silence for there to be music; that they must live ordinary lives; that they must have sameness in order that there be difference arising from their various geniuses; that is the nature of genius. "Just look at Guillaume de Machaut," they said, "a great man going under the guise of his name."

And from then on composers hid behind the sameness of them all having names given them by God.

(Sackbuts, Black Death)

For a performance of chance music, jongleurs, having found themselves quite by accident grouped on a stage in the auditorium of a museum, prepare to play an arrange-

A man and a woman growing against a warm wall

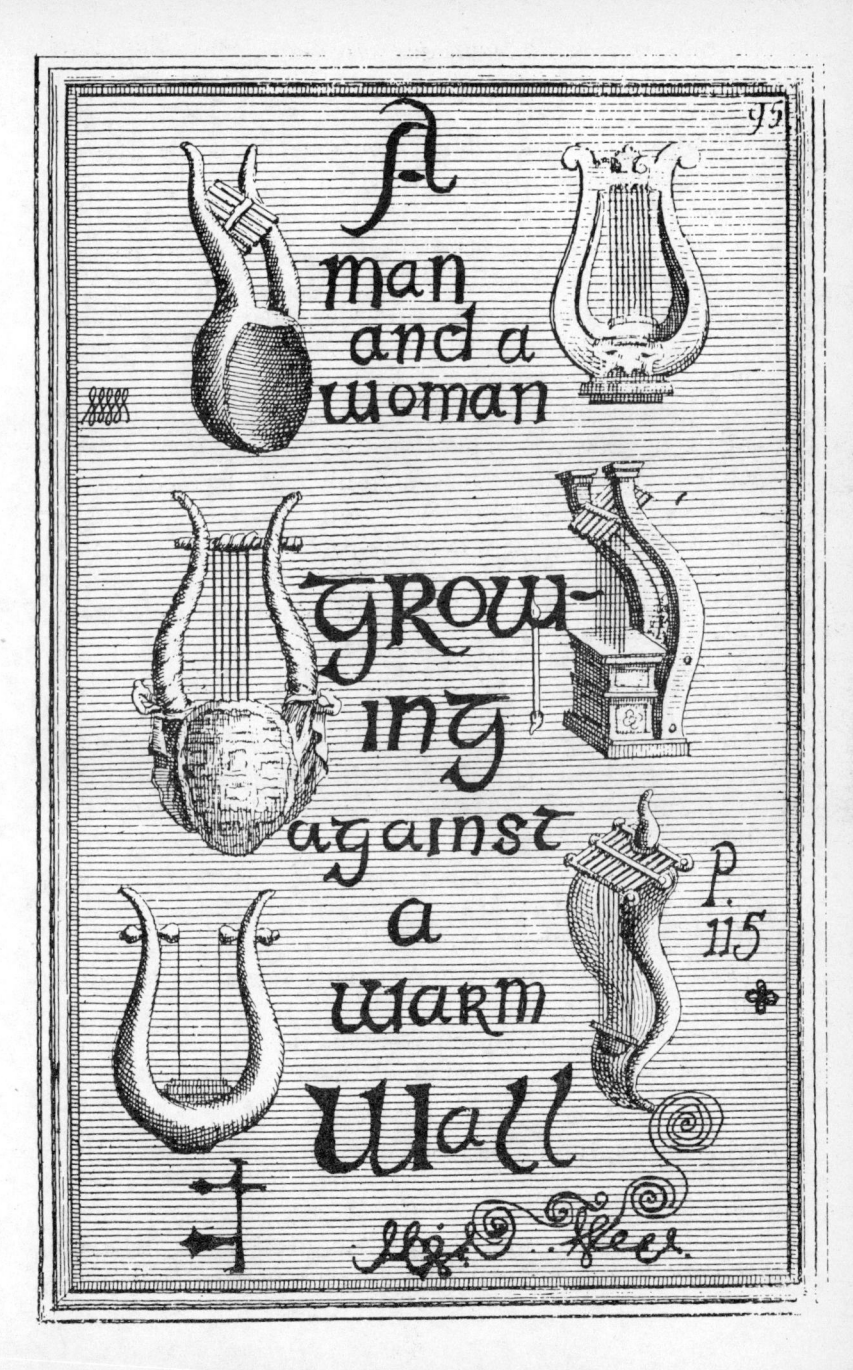

p. 115

ment of notes, the fruit of a motorway scored for sackbuts once plucked from a tree.

Perchance an audience is assembled in the proscenium. They applaud as the jongleurs file onto the stage with their sackbuts. The first jongleur clears his throat. "Um," he says several times, as though reciting a mantra. Then he announces that the jongleurs have a piece to play that would be greatly enhanced by the addition of a car. A member of the audience promptly leaps up on stage to hand over the keys to his Volvo, passing the curator on the way, whose mouth hangs open at the gall of the jongleurs. In the middle of a performance, what can he do? He sighs and shrugs his shoulders, leans back against a wall in the wings to smoke a cigarette.

Jongleurs are meanwhile explaining that the piece of music they are about to perform is written on a stave like a motorway stretching back to the Sixth Century, to Rome and to Gregory who first notated hearing.

"Gregory, how great thou art, is!" chants a jongleur, and the audience clap and cheer.

Several more men are persuaded to part with their cars. Men are keener than women, jongleurs notice. It doesn't occur to them that perhaps more men own cars. The jongleurs begin their performance gleefully with seventeen cars instead of seventeen sackbuts. They make white noise, all the notes of the spectrum, by driving backwards and forwards very fast.

The curator puts his head in his hands. The audience hear the white noise of the coloured cars they left home in to drive to the concert. On the road they were performers but now they find themselves in the passive role of the entertained.

The white noise bounces back from the soffits on the ceiling and fills the auditorium with a flow of traffic arranged into organum. The result is a resounding success and jongleurs consider themselves lucky. With chance music it is always a gamble. At the end of the performance the cars screech to a halt, the jongleurs stand and bow and the audience applaud wildly — they are starved for culture here. They stamp their feet and clap their hands, a deafening applause, and they are all deafened.

Then the audience comes forward to claim their cars for the drive home, but they find to their chagrin that instead of cars there are sackbuts. In the ensuing commotion in the carpark, the audience tries to insert keys into sackbuts to make them start, but the sackbuts can not, or will not, change their mode, and the use of keys is to no avail. Rather than leave empty-handed a concert arrived at in the possession of a car, the audience, to a man (literally), tucks a sackbut under one arm and marches off (passing a flummoxed troubadour along the way).

The astonished jongleurs, running out of the greenroom where they have been mopping their brows and gathering their breath and clapping each other on the back, are just in time to see their sackbuts disappear.

"What of the cars?" asks a whining jongleur. But the residue of cars is no use to them because cars were no use in the Middle Ages. Jongleurs find themselves reverting to the privilege of their former selves before they left the castle to become vagabonds; they are left with nothing.

And this is the beginning of the reversal of ways, of happiness backed out of a garage suddenly into the path of an oncoming sadness.

How cold it is!
But it is almost
spring.

(Hildegard entertaining the theologians)

In a thought the size of a cell or a concert hall, Hildegard, of the Mixolydian Mode and of the Twelfth Century and of the phosphorescent seams of faith discovered in darkness, now turned her attention to the scholars and theologians who had come to observe her and who stood gathered about her bed.

They had once been entertainers, professional storytellers along the numerous roads leading to Rome. But by the magic of Hildegard, her sleight-of-hand with visions like ribbons or white rabbits, she had become the entertainer, leaving the former performers no other role than that of the audience. Volmar and Richardis danced attendance on the visitors, and Hildegard, who had once known, but now pondered the contents of the ceiling of her cell, opened her mouth and a great babble — all musics, or white noise — issued from it, barely decipherable, only attainable for the price of a guess.

And the scholars and theologians opened their eyes wide blinding Hildegard with their light, thus preventing her from seeing, forcing her to wonder. And they listened to the pearls of wisdom that fell from her lips and scrabbled on the floor stringing them into decades.

First of all Hildegard told of the similarities of a garden, a sheep and a pearl to humans, and the scholars and theologians nodded sagely to show that they had always suspected there was this sameness. Whereupon Hildegard remarked there was difference in all things, that same and different were the same thing, or they were very different, one or the other. "The inside of the head is the same as the outside," said Hildegard. "And a woman's body is a wooden frame, strung, to be plucked like an Aeolian harp hung in a tree; and she has thin skin so the infant in her womb can get air." (She once wrote a medical treatise, *Causae et Curae*, in unscholarly Latin, taken down in dictation from the voice of God.)

"In a word," she went on, "there are sound, goodness and breathing." (And Vivaldi, during an asthma attack, inhaled deeply of notes and thus became an amphibian.) *"Word stands for the body, but the symphony stands for the spirit,"* said Hildegard. "And a musical performance will soften even the hardest heart, and divine love will trample on the dischord of the devil, and the cosmos and music are one, and through the power of hearing God reveals the hidden mysteries of the choirs of angels who in turn praise God."

All this Volmar recorded. The scholars and theologians, not used to such confines, could barely contain their astonishment within the walls of the cell. And Hildegard, disregarding the blankness of her ceiling (after all, in her more lucid moments she wrote blank verse) but entertaining the scholars and theologians just the same, put her hand to her head in a gesture of seeing, or of headache, because there was such wondering. And the scholars and theologians, seeing this pose, cried, "Hildegard indeed has the Gift!" And a garden, a sheep and a pearl nodded their heads in agreement.

(The manhole in the street)

Their real passion is the sackbut and if they had their way they would spend their lives as jongleurs in the South of France. But they do not have their way; what is this world if not the divergence of ways? (All leading towards the same point.) Since the reincarnation of sackbuts into cars and the resulting loss of the means of their livelihood (such as it was), china princes, to make ends meet, have found themselves a job working with a gang of men on the roads. Their task is to make china roses for the lids of manholes. The roses are useful because the lids no longer have to be prised off, and also they are very decorative. The problem with the roses is that they get chipped by the feet of people passing in the street. "Nothing is simple," says one of the china princes, wiping his brow as he surveys the lunchtime crowd.

The shoes are all different, yet to china princes, viewing them from ground level, they become a blur. "Here is a great paradox," says another china prince, "that when people are trying to be different they are the same, and when they are the same they are different." This he intones leaning on what he bluntly calls his shovel. As it is against the regulations of the Ministry of Works to lean on one's shovel, due to workmen falling asleep and putting their eyes out, the foreman rushes over to admonish the china prince.

(An adventure repeats itself, a difference included)

Their name was Land or The Laying on of Hands and they lived not only hand to mouth but also land to eye; in all things, a measure of their usefulness the laying on of eyes.

They longed to live where they could see Land and they renounced the orderliness of the suburbs to do this. Leaving the intervals between streets, the places that are not drawn on maps but are, nevertheless, where people dwell, they moved to the Land and they continued to live on the Land all through the encroachment of one age upon another. As far as they knew, order reigned in the rest of the world, in the suburbs of Auckland, in the corrugations of the sky. And the windows of houses sealed the sky in a glass case to preserve it. But the Lands knew it was the current orderliness of the world that allowed them to leave it for the Land, to leave knowing for wondering.

When a Coke can landed one day on their property, thrown in anger by a traveller who had lost his way and found himself between everything, nowhere to be found on a map, the Lands were astonished by this object, by its beauty, and also its ugliness when they discovered they could cut themselves on it.

The next day another can, exactly the same, was thrown onto the Land. The Lands, assuming that the nature of objects was that there was only one of them (knowing nothing of canning operations, supermarkets, or Andy Warhol), considered this replicated object, discussed it, and concluded there were three possible explanations for its presence.

One was that time had turned around and was going backwards. Another was that two people had made the same object, unwittingly, just as the same myths were created unknowingly in different parts of the world. The third was that there were now many Coke cans in the world, that the world was in fact made of Coke cans, like atoms and that was why skyscrapers were so shiny and able to sway to and fro in the wind or an earthquake, and that was how cars had been taught to roll over and play dead. The Lands didn't solve this riddle and it remained one of the great mysteries, the things they wondered about in the evening.

Until one Sunday, that is, when on an excursion to the church of St Gregory of the Holy Neume twenty miles away, the Lands noticed there were Coke cans scattered along the roadside, and that there were also people, their houses, cars, animals and children cluttering the sides of this same road. And there was a dotted line defining the (middle) of the road, traffic exceeding the speed of sound either side of it, where there had once been one Landrover, the Lands'.

The Lands returned home from Mass, their children sipping Coke on the back seat, to discover that a small city had sprung up where they had contemplated planting the new translation of the *Tao Te Ching*, that there was scaffolding clinging to the trees, a telephone line to the New York Stock Exchange, and traffic lights where two Lands, each making a visit to the dunny in the middle of the night, had once bumped into each other.

The Lands wailed, "There are people all over the Land, and the Dark Ages are getting increasingly Middle Aged, they are spreading everywhere and now they are saying there was even Enlightenment in the Middle Ages! Where will it end?"

They once had a problem with blackberry, the Lands, when they first moved to the Land, but they cut it back, not completely, but so there would be just enough for a dozen pots of blackberry jam in a season, to embellish bread, but not to take the place of bread. And the blackberry, scythed, became a quiet neighbourhood in a corner of the universe.

They have always preferred the Dark Ages and that is where they have lived, aware at the same time it was the leftovers of the Age of Enlightment that allowed them to live as they pleased. Now, ironically, a return to the systems of the Middle Ages has wrested them from their Dark Ages and brought them screaming and kicking into the Twentieth Century. However, they do not scream, neither do they kick. The Lands, with a healthy respect for the elements, typical of their time, see immediately that the advance of the Middle Ages revisited is too much for an Ars Antiqua scythe drawn across the surface of the Land, and they go quietly into this new age.

(*La Messiaen de Notre Dame*)

A composer of this church
one Sunday attending

the Mass of his belief or
equation to explain his

worldly possession, said
A large symphony when they

passed him the plate.
One quartet, several symphonic

poems, a Mass for eight sopranos
Choruses for Joan of Arc and

Twenty Visions of the Infant Jesus.
He said *Thank you I have already*

given. He had taken the triad
filled in between its notes

so the triad was no longer
thrown into relief, each

tone of the twelve-tone scale
was heard just as often as its

brothers and sisters — serial
music for an installation

of socialism. He was
a passionist, organist at the Church of

the Holy Trinity, professor of harmony
at the Paris Conservatoire, a teacher

of rhythm there, he taught

the difference between
three beats per measure in the

Middle Ages and the
rhythmic modes of the Twentieth

Century, between the snapping
and snarling of Wolf Fifths

and the judicious use of
diminished intervals. Messiaen

was a composer of *musique
concrète*, the bell of the birdcall

caught in a tree, contained
in a concert hall. A dove

once flew beneath the wall-
less roof of the Tanglewood

Music Centre (the music of
the perimeter escaping)

and this dove warmed with
the fluttering of its feathers

the rosin of the bows of the
violinists who played, then

with feeling. And Messiaen said
The message of the dove is divine

inspiration. The *musique concrète*
of this the next world contained

in this. In a musical dictionary
the *Oxford Companion,* Messiaen

comes after The Messiah by
Handel or The Messiah by God.

(A bull in northern China)

For china princes who have worked in a china factory it is a small matter to walk into a cake shop in their lunch hour, and everything is the matter. A swan, a bell, a rose, a blue ribbon tied in a bow — nothing is the exception and nothing is out of the ordinary. Except that the woman behind the counter insists on china princes buying a cake after they have strolled across it. Her insistence is a large ornate thing and china princes are very struck with it, but all the same they walk out of the shop as fast as their little legs will carry them.

(and Japan)

At the perimeter of the universe can be heard the music of a mode of transport — the monorail system of Tokyo. Sound waves, commuting, set up conditions similar to those found inside the traditional *shakuhachi* or flute. The trains are jammed with people, standing room only. They shuttle back and forth like the "standing waves" that operate in the flute when an almost continuous flow of breath enters the aperture and commutes along the narrow chamber. In this way the flute makes the music of God. The music of the mode of transport has a divine slowness perceptible only at the perimeter of the universe by the ear of God, his angels, dead souls, and a woman suspended in a divine dream.

She is passive, oh how
passive she is!
She is so passive she cannot be
ignored, a persimmon
waiting to be
plucked
that might
at any moment
fall from a great height.

(Massenet chalks a circle round the female lead)

His belief was in beauty rather than in God. This, of course, was the French way. He wrote operas with women as lead characters, his favourite the figure of the reformed courtesan, as in *Marie-Magdeleine*. Indeed, all his heroines clung to a religious eroticism rather than a virtue. With these operas he was wildly popular, popular as opera was with the French.

But in *Le Jongleur de Notre Dame* he broke new ground. He wrote an opera with a cast entirely of men, apart from two angels in the final scene, who could as well be boys as high sopranos. There was not a woman to be seen or heard. Members of the Opera Society, eavesdropping on rehearsals, threw up their hands and cried, "What has happened to Massenet's heroines?" They had come to expect them. And concerned agents asked on behalf of their female clients, *"Où est la femme?"* In reply, Massenet would only smile cryptically.

The story of Our Lady's Juggler he had taken from a Medieval miracle play, rewritten for theatre by Anatole France. It is of a jongleur, at first degenerate, who converts to Catholicism and enters a monastery. And a monastery, while a fine place for plainsong, was a strange setting for a French opera, especially one by the virgin/whore-complexed Massenet. Nevertheless Massenet proceeded with Plot and he proceeded with Passion, while leaving out the very element that had driven his other works. And the men in the chorus and in the lead roles of the opera shrugged their shoulders and said, *"Comme si, comme ça, il est Massenet."*

At the first performance opera-goers came from far and wide to hear what Massenet had produced this time, and they sat in the darkness of the proscenium and listened to the tenors, baritones and basses, and to the two boy sopranos who took the roles of the angels, and they felt a great absence, as if the opera was a perimeter made around the thing it was really about.

Afterwards at supper in a fashionable brasserie, Massenet asked his friends, "So, did you hear her? She is inbetween notes. She is inbetween Plot and inbetween Passion."

His friends, not wanting to be thought insensitive or stupid, clapped Massenet on the back or kissed his cheek and said, *"Oui, oui, la femme, elle était magnifique!"*

Meanwhile, critics scribbling down reviews hurriedly in deserted newspaper offices, wrote dissertations on the poignancy of the female role, disregarding the men who had sung their hearts out.

And though no one had seen her, by no one had she been heard, the female lead stalked through all their dreams.

(All weathers, except summer)

They are getting terribly chipped; a bump on the head, the end knocked off a nose, the loss of a shard of hair. And their clothes — their china hats and coats and ties and the beautiful Chinese sleeves she ironed carefully, and their waistcoats — look what has become of them! They are perfectly ruined like the perfection imperfection has made of the ruins of ancient Rome.

China princes find themselves inappropriately dressed for the weather, the rain of feet, and for the noise jackhammers make. By the middle of the afternoon it is all such a problem for china princes used to the simple life of a vagabond, a jongleur, the tedium of a china factory and the games they invented there, that they walk off the job. They have failed their own physical condition. Their physical condition is described as no such thing by the ever-decreasing foreman watching them go.

(On the Land and on Queen St)

It was once the Land but now it is the city. On their way down Queen St a procession of china princes meets a procession of Lands and they all stop in the middle of the street to talk. They take up so much room with their talking that the other pedestrians, skirting around them, their trousers, shout for them to shove over and stop creating a hazard. But there are so many Lands of all ages and so many china princes of all shapes and sizes that it is impossible to budge them and so, there in the middle of the street, they are reacquainted.

The last time they met was as jongleurs entertaining the Lands in the Hokianga, before the Lands moved to the city and the city to the Lands, and jongleurs succumbed to the inexorable march of devolution — the loss of their sackbuts, etc.

"But we thought you were still itinerant musicians!" cry the Lands. China princes explain that they had a change of fortunes, unfortunately, that their sackbuts were repossessed, ghosted, and they have been forced to find other employment. But they are still maintaining their good spirits, their numerical order and their china bodies, which have always come in handy.

The Lands then inquire discreetly after the multifarious boxes of possessions they remember sending back into the sky from the Land when the jongleurs came to visit. "Now that we've had time to think about it, from the 'burbs, so to speak, we think we might have been a bit hasty in...um ..."

"Condemning the bourgeois?" supply china princes.

The Lands hesitate. "Well, we still have our beliefs," they say. "But we are now much in need of possessions — you see, this is the way it is here." And they spread their hands to indicate the shops of Queen St, the nothingness of the land.

"Sadly, one of the crates came open," reply china princes (jemmied more likely, is their private opinion), "and consequently a whole host of our possessions are floating in space." All cast their eyes heavenwards. "The rest of the stuff, well, we're not quite sure what has become of it — we've become less and less materialistic in our travels, you'll be pleased to hear. We travel light. Perhaps one day, though, we'll get our pigeons back."

"We thought the pigeons were hired," remark the Lands.

To which china princes reply, "Well yes, but not more so than anything." Oh the difficulties of possessions, their disappearances and reappearances like a house squatted in by unwelcome ghosts, coming and going, coming and ghost-writing a novelette!

"The difficulty of everything!"

"There is always a problem."

The Lands advise a visit to an encounter-tenor of their acquaintance who once had insurmountable problems, now mounted and ridden away across a plain. Having belief in chance, the *Tao Te Ching*, the encounter-tenor adapted the ancient Chinese practice of throwing three coins of the same denomination in the air for guidance, much like a hopeless display of hands.

"He throws three notes into the air and listens to the way they Land," says the Lands.

And the way they land is, in the way of atoms, a solution.

The Lands then report that since their move to the city, lock, stock and station agent, they have moved into a little flat with glass windows, and through these windows they watch an exhibition of everything in this world. And they have discovered that, yes, it is almost real.

"You could stretch out your hand and touch it, were it not for the glass," say the Lands.

Following urban pursuits they have just bought a ticket in a competition for the price of a guess — how many pedestrians can fit in a jar? At one time they spent their evenings pondering how many angels could dance on the head of a pin, but the question was very difficult and they never found the answer, at least not by the means of wondering. Compared to angels, the problem of how many pedestrians are in the jar will be much more easily solved. "A piece of cake," say the Lands.

Promising to consult the encounter-tenor and counting heads, respectively, china princes and the Lands make their farewells and go their separate ways, and darkness and light flood back into the street.

(The Counter Reformation and the Difficulty of the Virgin: after *A History of Western Music*)

There was the sack of Rome but then there was the retaliation. Rome was alarmed at losing England and much of northern Europe to the long arm of the Reformation. The Council of Trent was called to right this wrong. The Council of Trent went on for a long time, from 1545 to 1563. A young man coming to maturity was the age of the Council of Trent. A woman was of marriageable age when she had reached the age of the Council of Trent.

The council addressed, among other things, the current laxity in music, which perhaps was responsible for the Reformation itself — in particular, the use of polyphony, many voices singing the text which obscured the text, and this text, after all, was the word of God. And the Council denounced the barbarism of instruments in church, and the profanity of Parody Masses, which were based on secular melodies. It was thought that the music to the glory of God should return to purity, for instance, that embodied in the Masses of Guillaume de Machaut.

Music was faced with a witch hunt, a seeking out of the many spells and charms of polyphony. But it must be said, polyphony *had* gone a little haywire.

There appeared, then, another composer. Giovanni Pierluigi da Palestrina was his name. Now Palestrina, composing in the midst of this cold front created by opposing pressures, the Reformation and the Counter Reformation, wrote a Mass for six voices to demonstrate that there could be polyphony to the glory of the God and towards the elucidation of the text. He called this Mass *Missa Papae*

Marcellus, after the Pope of the day. And this Mass was indeed polyphonic and it was indeed very beautiful — and yes, it was lucid. The word of God shone out from the interweaving of the six voices. And the Pope of the day said, "Bravo! Palestrina has saved us!"

This was how Palestrina became known as the saviour of Church music, because he salvaged it not only from the embroidery of the Reformation but also from the lunatic purity of the Council of Trent.

Keeping within the dictum of the council, which was that the "impure or lascivious" in music be avoided, Palestrina became the most important composer of the Counter Reformation. He shunned the complicated chromaticisms of his more worldly contemporaries and employed only the few alterations of *musica ficta* demanded by the imperfection of physics. Beset by these limitations, a containing of vision, he nevertheless went on to compose 102 Masses, 450 motets, 56 spiritual madrigals, and 83 secular madrigals.

(Addressing the dream)

A tightwire to trip
comets and angels and strung
with the hand-washed limbs of a man
pegged out to dry in the prevailing
musics. Oh how I like
piano concertos! he said and
whereas comments like that would
once have annoyed her, now she finds
she cannot live without them.
And she can not sleep.
She dreams but she does not
sleep, loves but does not wake.
A love walks in the wakefulness of ships
and her love has transported her here
like a mode of transport or of
music — Dorian, Aeolian, Mixolydian —
ingredients of the fall of atoms

the inevitable mix of the way the universe
is. Oh how
a season will not change when bidden!
The will of seasons is such that nothing will
bend them. She touched
a dream dressed in the objects
that desire it, wearing
the limbs of a man to keep out the cold
or to invite it in from the cold, his
warmth she can no longer
tell from her own or tell it
anything. A difference has made no
difference, only a sameness and
what she has imagined.
She once read a novelette
and thought she had dreamt it.

(Not wanting to go through the looking-glass)

China princes have a small crusade upon a piano, but this is not an adventure.

    In the personal column of a newspaper an elderly woman has advertised that she would like to have her piano played, a laying on of hands. It is not good for a piano to go unplayed for any length of time, the time conducted by the absence of hands. China princes, in need of amusement, also having hands they must soon lay upon something — a piano, a sackbut, be that as it may — apply in person at the stated address dressed in their china finery and with the tips of their fingers dipped in gold.

    The elderly woman, appearing at the front door etched with a flight of swallows, is delighted that not one but seventeen musicians have come to entertain her. She ushers them into her sitting room, departs momentarily and returns with afternoon tea, all dressed up in the fur teaset she received as a wedding present sixty years ago when they were the fashion.

    "It was my husband," she says wistfully, "who played the piano."

But one day, fifty-nine years ago, he left her hurriedly, much as a felt-tipped hammer leaves the string it has just touched.

"Such escapades! An escape artist, he was," says the woman indulgently, catching a few tears with a lace handkerchief. "How great thou art!" she sighs, raising her eyes heavenwards (and what does she see?)

China princes, not used to such an exhibition of emotion, quickly bring the lips of their moustachioed cups to the rims of their mouths. They are feeling nervous and must have something to do with their hands. For her part the elderly woman has found it less painful to have nothing to do with them, with her hands.

Showing them into a room containing a piano and a glass-fronted cabinet full of miniature china ornaments, the elderly woman pauses, puts her head on one side and mutters to herself, "There is something about their bodies, the way they move, a particular persuasion on walking across a room." When china princes look self-conscious, she adds aloud, "I can't quite put my finger on it, but I will tell you in due course." She then retires to the balcony.

China princes, left to their own devices, play Mozart sonatas, complete with the ornaments between notes, until well on in the afternoon. Their only movement for several hours is between one movement and the next. That there are many of them, china princes, is not a problem. There is always a problem, apart from this long moment which is not one, nor this movement for that matter, and it does — matter. Many hands make light work, especially where polyphony is concerned, and also in the handling of chords. The stretch of a hand across the keyboard, barely an octave for small hands, is increased to the required ten or eleven notes when the hand of another china prince is enlisted.

In the early evening, the room full to the brim with the notes of an afternoon of Mozart, tired china princes get up from the piano, stretch, and walk directly across to where they see a china cabinet against the wall. It is filled with the most extravagant display of china ornaments, a flowering to match the sumptuousness of the elderly woman's emotions — twice that; the cabinet is backed with mirrors so it is in fact twice as full as it might otherwise have been. China princes make muffled cries of astonishment, remembering their days in the china factory engaged in the manufacture of the figurines. They gingerly slide the glass door of the cabinet across and begin fingering the ornaments: ballerinas, shepherds, a string quartet of monkeys in red vests, baskets full of roses, single china shoes the size a fairy might wear, and living-room furniture complete with piano. The oohs and aahs of the china princes frost up the glass.

The elderly woman, appearing from the balcony when she hears the piano stop, hearing it even though it has stopped, casts her hands into the air — her empty hands, an emptiness caused by a flight of swallows on the front door taking the notes of a piano with them in their beaks — and she cries, "I couldn't put my finger on it, but now my finger has been placed upon it!" And she declares that seventeen china princes are exactly what she has been wanting for the exhibition in her cabinet. "Not seventeen, but thirty-four," she corrects herself, remembering the looking-glass in which the ornaments survey their own image. Whereupon she begins to finger with delight the bodies of the china princes, the exquisite mould of their coats and hats and ties, and of their sleeves and waistcoats and also, as they had made a special effort to dress for the occasion, the froth of china lace at their wrists and necks, the gold buckles of their shoes, the ornate curves of their gold hair and the tips of their fingers dipped in gold.

With a force seemingly given her by God or by the weight of 250 000 copies of the personal column of the newspaper, the elderly woman tries to push the china princes into the cabinet, saying at the same time enticingly, "Look, there is a small piano inside for you to play!"

But although there was a time when nothing would have pleased china princes more than the company of china ornaments contained on a shelf in the sky, now the idea of the china cabinet horrifies them. It is not so much the china objects that disturb them, as the sight of themselves in the mirror behind: a man, singular, present, of human flesh and with an expression of outrage upon his face.

China princes blanch in shock. Did they not become a prince all those years ago to avoid precisely this circumstance? Did they not take up the sackbut, leave the castle and join the jongleurs, becoming many of them, to prevent this? And then, of the need to make ends meet and finding themselves working in a china factory, did they not adapt their bodies to those that spilled off the production line and become ornaments, in order that they could live between notes like the byways of Mozart? Did they not perfect all this for the express purpose of avoiding a certain vision — themselves (themself) (himself)?

(Herself?) Now the elderly woman, crotchety and quavering, is losing patience. She engages in a hand-to-hand tussle with one of the china princes in an effort to force him into the cabinet.

The china prince cries, "We can't possibly do this — we are made of china!" As that makes no impact, another china prince says, "I like piano concertos," but that is no more to the point, considering there is a tiny china piano just the far side of the glass and it is waiting to be played, and also its reflection is waiting for a travelling musician to sit down at its keyboard and make the reflection of notes.

All else failing, china princes, with an Herculean display of their heels, run out through the etched door as fast as their china bodies will allow them, releasing as they go a flight of swallows that has been confined there for thirty years.

(The tenor of their ways)

There is only one problem but there are many china princes. The problem therefore has many inversions. Sackbuts are sometimes a problem, the absence of them. The novelette, its age, that too, on particular days, is a problem. Anything can be a problem if you let it, is the opinion of china princes and, this being so, they engage the services of an encounter-tenor.

He was once a choirboy in the Vatican City, this before the custom of castrating boy sopranos had been dispensed with. His voice was of such beauty that everything shall be given for it, and everything was. And the encounter-tenor, bereft, forsaken, took all the music of the Catholic Church, from Gregory I (the Great) to Messiaen, to his name and these musics became his children and he was the father of a large progeny. Then one day as he was performing in the Sistine Chapel and looking up at the fruit of his seed (four hundred million notes upon a page) displayed in abundance on the curve of a ceiling, he realised that he had not opened his eyes and what he saw was the miraculous reflection of his wishes.

With that the disenchanted encounter-tenor left the Church and abandoned his many children to the Vatican orphanages, and now he is running encounter sessions for people who believe they have insurmountable problems. It is the encounter-tenor's creed that no problem is without its solution.

China princes, in their first session, blurt out in a counterpoint of versions that there are many points of view but there is only one woman and they love her more than anything, and that is the matter with everything.

The encounter-tenor says shyly that he, also, has not been without love.

V

Dreaming and Seeing: The Fifth Season and the Art of No Such Thing

(A season laid fallow)

China princes go to Hungary, of all places. It is the end of the Earth, but it is the end of the Nineteenth Century and it is the place to go as far as innovative music is concerned. While drinking in a tavern in Budapest they meet a group of composers who introduce themselves as Bartók, Janáček, Kondály, et al. The composers are down-at-heel, but interesting. China princes tell them that they themselves were once musicians, jongleurs, until they lost their instruments. Hearing this, the composers lean closer and inform their new friends in low voices that for quite some time they have been engaged in a search. China princes lean forward. "What are you looking for?" they ask.

Janáček answers. "Ze fifz beat," he says complicitly, "ze long-lost beat to ze bar, we belief could exeest just out off earshot. Haf you seen him?"

China princes look at each other blankly, raise their palms and shake their heads. "Search me," says the littlest, after drawing on his beer.

The composers explain that they've looked everywhere. They've scoured the city, sent a search party into the country with a scalloped edge of torches, and generally kept an ear to the ground, but to no avail.

"But why a fifth beat?" ask china princes. "Aren't four enough?"

The Hungarian composers exchange amused glances. "In answer to ze question," begins Bartók, "one-two-three-four-fife . . ." And the composers sing a folk song, keeping rhythm with the fingers of one hand.

"Zo," says Bartók at the end of the song, "you see we haf fife beats in ze bar, okay? But only zo far, in folk song. This is fery nice. But it is all fery well. Me and my friends here," (here he inclines his head towards Janáček, Kodály, et al.) "vat ve vant is for the fife beats to be in, how-you-say, classical music. Zerious, written-down music. Music zo complicated you can't remember it 'less you write it down. Okay?"

"Okay," say the china princes.

China princes join in the search. First they look in bus terminals and zoos and churches and picture theatres, behind the seats among lolly wrappers. But to no avail. Then they try parks and museums and cafes and convents. Then supermarkets, the freezer section. Then in the long grass between the arms of zigzags.

Then one china prince says, "This is no good, where is the least likely place the fifth beat would be?"

Between them they decide that the least likely place for the fifth beat of the bar would be the most likely place — where old things are stored. And they begin looking in dusty attics. They look in all the dusty attics in Budapest, and finally, in the last dusty attic, whimpering in a trunk, they find the long-lost beat, weak but still breathing.

China princes rush to Bartók, Janáček, Kodály, et al., who are looking depressed, dropping over their vodkas in the tavern. "We've found it! We've found it!" shout the china princes.

The composers immediately set upon it with delight, slapping each other on the back, tears streaming down their faces. "Oh Janáček!" "Oh Bartók!" "Oh Kodály!" they cry. "Oh mercy mine! Ze fifz beat! Oh mysterious exeestence off ze outer reaches off ze bar!" And forgetting china princes entirely, they set the fifth beat to music, serious music in need of being written down.

It wasn't long before the fifth beat was made known throughout eastern Europe and there was much rejoicing.

For people in the West, however, when the news trickled out, the discovery of the fifth beat was quite beyond them. There was great consternation (and still is!) at this oddness like the oddness of an extra limb. What had once been three-beats-per-measure to the glory of the Trinity, then four beats, to the scandal of the Church but at least it was like the seasons — suddenly now there were five, as the music of what was once called the Eastern Bloc joined the doxology of the great composers (Western).

Just as East meets West, wondering meets knowing, and what is discovered must first be imagined (this, certainly, in the world of science (its *world*), the laboratory, where the much-heralded meetings of famous atoms take place, they embrace, are photographed and cabled to the metropolitan dailies around the world (the *world*)); and leaps of faith land on the magic carpets of equations.

And so it was, following the enlightenment of the fifth beat, that the existence of a fifth season was considered.

China princes had been cast aside by the Hungarian composers who left the tavern for their very own garrets and now cared nothing but for scribbling down furiously the pent-up five-beat music within them.

"That's okay. We understand," said the china princes. Did they themselves not pursue the *Ficta* with the same gusto on occasion? Did they not find themselves in Hungary at the end of the Nineteenth Century for that very purpose? "The Hungarian composers, all *they* have to do is shut themselves in their garrets," said china princes, not without envy.

This, then, was what happened: They once found winter, the fourth season, revelled in it, splashed about in it, and released the secular tinkle of minute icicles into the liturgical year. Four challenged the Trinity, and four-beats-per-measure was soon heard even in churches, the former strongholds of threesomes. And winter became de rigueur amongst jongleurs. Now, seeing there were five beats, china princes began to suspect the presence of a fifth-season, that is, or time of year. And they theorised on the nature of it, its contours, in order to lay tracks for a train of thought through twelve months.

"A fifth season," expounded the tallest, leanest, most bearded china prince, leaning on the bar in Budapest and raising his hand for another beer, "left lying fallow for so long — since before the Dark Ages, when there was something darker than dark — a fifth season would've had time to gather much goodness to itself in the way of minerals and trace elements, china shards, discarded notes — the perfection that comes of ruined imperfection — so much goodness that it would be able to produce a cabbage the size of a room, a room the size of a house and a house the size of a host of thoughts!"

And these thoughts once wondering would now be knowing.

The other china princes, elbowing for room at the bar, lent an ear indulgently to their friend.

"And because everything is linked," continued the guru china prince, now well-oiled with alcohol, "(there is nothing that is not linked), the fifth season would be allied to the circle of fifths of Pythagorus, which has always been there — a little imperfect, admittedly, but there all the same — unknown until Pythagorus imagined it, and then it was made known."

"Bravo!"

In the same way as Pythagorus imagining, china princes have made a leap of faith across an arc etched in air.

Meanwhile Bartók, Janáček, Kodály, et al., shivering in their respective garrets, warmed themselves by the drumming of the fingers of one hand.

(A magic realist hazards a guess)

It is indeed almost summer. China princes, as they continue down Queen St after leaving the Lands, come across a clown dressed in the lightness of her everyday costume, a small gathering of people who admire her antics. She has clothed herself in her audience; it is almost warm.

But china princes, much preferring the cold and pretending it is cold, hunch their shoulders and are preparing to shuffle off down the street when they are waylaid by the clown in the habit of clowns, and also of cats, and also of

And there is the minutest thrill among everything in the Universe

page 127
CXXXII
Sonagli adoprati nella Chiesa.

certain people, of desiring the attention of those who ignore them; no other will do.

"If you please, gentlemen!" she says. "Could you spare a ten dollar note for a trick? It will be returned to you."

China princes, disgruntled but watched by an audience of expectant pedestrians, riffle through their various pockets and pouches and eventually find up a sleeve something they had always thought was an autumn leaf but which turns out to be a ten dollar note, fallen once in a domain, and this they hand to the clown.

Without further ado the clown seals the note in an envelope. Then she produces another envelope, displays its emptiness, seals it, and shuffles the two envelopes together. She then lights a match and sets fire to one of the envelopes. The small crowd is now a big crowd. Their oohs and aahs are enough to blow out the flame, so the clown lights another match and this time the envelope is allowed to burn furiously. Holding the taper between her teeth like a cigarette, she opens the other envelope.

With great alacrity, her magic astonishing the whole crowd, the clown puts out the flames on the last inch of the envelope she held in her mouth. "Kind sirs — a portion of your ten dollar note," she says with a flourish.

Jongleurs left bereft once more, it is more than they can take, and to a man, they burst into tears. The clown puts her hand to her mouth in a gesture of self-doubt. You may think this story is made up, but in fact it is true.

(A dominion to sleep under)

And Hildegard of the Twelfth Century and of the gift of tears rent in garments, and of the lines in the palm of her hand transfigured onto the ceiling, found before long that the convent attached to the monastery of St Disibod was filling up at an alarming rate with postulants. They came to follow the seasons of her visions, winters; and they occupied every cell with their dividing and their subdividing into same but different; and they spilled out into the corridors and cloisters, the warm-walled garden, and the recesses that were tucks let out of the main chapel and their beds were ledges perched near the ceiling.

Back home in the towns and villages where the young postulants had come from, a generation of men faced lives alone, their future wives gone to die in a war of dominions. But instead of pining they turned to and learned cooking and sewing and how to roll newspapers into logs for the fire. And heavy industry now took place in the evenings, the men seated before a roaring blaze.

Meanwhile Hildegard, perceiving a need and now more confident of her powers of persuasion, repeated her request to Kuno, Abbot of St Disibod's, for a convent to be built at Rupertsburg opposite Bingen am Rhein. The sight, she reiterated, had come to her in a vision, the site marked by a pin in a map. And angels were dancing upon them, but Hildegard said the place for the convent was not where any of these pins was, but between one pin and another. "Because on the site where the pin was, was there not already a pin?" she asked Kuno rhetorically.

Despite the vision, Kuno would not agree to the move. The exorbitant cost of convents concerned him. "A community of the unworldly," he remarked drily to Hildegard, "consumes many worldly goods." But perhaps it was more that he was reluctant to lose the woman whose powers had put St Disibod's on the map. When Hildegard cited the map in her head ("the inside of the head is the same as the outside," she said), its pins, Kuno replied, "I can hear a pin drop," and that was the end of that.

He knew, however, he swam against a tide of popular opinion, like a salmon leaping upstream to spawn. Also against the unmistakable tide of women leaving a watermark close to the very ceiling of the famous visionary.

Then Hildegard called upon a higher authority. Not yet God but Heinrich, Archbishop of Mainz. She declared in one of her famous letters, "Archbishop, so overcrowded are the conditions here, that if I do not have my convent at Bingen soon, my visions will begin turning in on themselves. Thus befalls goodness confined: a confinement of forty years, the length of the generation of monsters, if not given space, will produce a beast who will roam throughout Christendom seeking whom he may devour." Hildegard sat back and waited with her postulants for the Archbishop's reply.

He replied in person, visiting the celebrated cell, his large body draped from head to foot in purple, an expression of foreboding peeping out from the folds. Seeing a chink in the bishopric armour, Hildegard put her hand to her temple, a gesture of the strain of so many women and so many winters all in a row.

And the Archbishop, observing the gesture and worrying about the monster, said, "Hildegard indeed has the Gift of Headache!"

(The benefactor on the Left Bank)

Suffering the tiredness of those who dream but do not sleep, missing the ordinariness of the woman, her oeuvre and the cult they had created around her (therefore, *their* oeuvre or body of work) — they are just about to call upon the services of homing pigeons once again to transport their possessions back where they came from, when they meet, quite by chance, a woman who can offer them what they most desire.

At the time of the introduction they are sitting astride the bough of a tree in the Bois de Boulogne, and this bough is being sawn off by an undergardener. China princes are making notes in a notebook for the *Ficta*; but really they have no idea what should happen next and though they constantly send out flares from their ears, hoping to catch the attention of a passing dove, they are not visited by inspiration. For as long as they care to remember they have been halfway through a sentence, at its comma.

As if to tempt fate — anyway to break with the tradition of sentences — the bough parts company with the tree and one of the china princes, the one who held forth in the tavern in Budapest, now clutching the notebook, falls into the lap of a woman sitting on a bench below. The other china princes teeter on the blunt end of the branch, unsure whether it is best to let themselves drop into the woman's lap as well, or to hang there like quavers waiting to be played.

"Hello," says the woman to the fallen china prince, "my name is Sylvia Beach."

"I'm the china prince," says the china prince.

"And I'm the Emperor of Japan," returns Sylvia, throwing up her hands in a Chrysanthemum Dynasty.

The china prince sees she is reading a little manuscript called *Pomes Peny-each*, and he nods towards it and smiles and mouths the title.

"It rhymes nicely with my name," says Sylvia. In her turn she notices the china prince has a notebook and she asks what it is.

"Oh, just my scribbling," he replies.

"Just our scribbling!" say the other china princes from above.

Sylvia's hearing flickers but she doesn't think to look up.

Then the first china prince adds with pride, "It is nine years old."

"It is eighty-one years old," chime the other china princes, at which the fallen china prince looks up and mouths, "Go away!"

"And it is called *Musica Ficta*," the first china prince smilingly tells Sylvia.

"*Musica Ficta?*" repeats Sylvia. But at that moment her attention is claimed by something in the distance china princes cannot see.

"Good day, Adrienne Monier!" calls Sylvia.

China princes peer closely in the direction of the returned greeting, and presently they can just make out the figure of a woman dressed entirely in grey, exactly the same colour as the paths of the Bois, a path moving across a path. She is rather heard than seen, the patter of her feet. But that patter! What a glorious sound it is! Or perhaps it is that there is no need for china princes to close their eyes to aid listening; there are distractions such as Adrienne Monier, seen. With a final wave, Sylvia remarks that her friend dresses in grey always, all ways, because it rhymes with her name.

When Sylvia turns her thoughts back to the matter at hand she has a proposition. It appears she has been looking for a writer, a novelist to be specific, to favour with the sound of her name, and she had been going to sponsor the author of *Pomes Peny-each* because it rhymes so nicely with Beach (and also another of his books, *Ulysses*, has some bearing on Sylvia). So if Beach rhymes with each, well, for that matter, Sylvia rhymes with ficta. "And it does matter," says Sylvia, "because our lives are conducted according to rhyme."

And also according to God, is her opinion. Sylvia believes that this china prince and his manuscript are a sign from above, what has befallen her. And such faith she has in what must not be ignored, that everything shall be given for it, and she says to the china prince who fell into her lap, "Come, I have something to give you".

China prince, transfixed, tucks the *Ficta* under his arm and follows Sylvia across the Seine to the Left Bank. The others follow at a discreet distance, discouraged whenever possible by the first china prince. The procession arrives at an *oubliette* on the top floor of a building overlooking the river, and here Sylvia installs them, the china prince and his nine-year-old manuscript.

"Sylvia, this is very nice," comments the single china prince.

"It can all be yours," says Sylvia.

When the china prince hears the other china princes scrabbling at the door to get in he recognises that they might pose a problem, the question of point of view and how many are required, and he decides it is best to be honest with Sylvia. There is also the little matter of the woman, no such thing, but the china prince rapidly arrives at the conclusion one honesty is more than enough for one day. He hesitates, then ventures, "On certain days — not often but sometimes — there may be, um, more of me than on other days. There is, as you might say, a pluralism in

our — my make-up, and occasionally it may be noticeable."
He waits anxiously for Sylvia's reply.

Sylvia pauses, sighs, smoothes her gloves. "I've often heard it said," she says, "that many hands make a light work of art. If that is the case with you and your ... friends, well, you had better look elsewhere for accommodation. I have no interest whatsoever in light entertainment. Moreover, I have another acquaintance by the name of Joyce who is experimenting with voice, but there is only one of him, and he would move in without delay were I to offer him the *oubliette*."

Her speech over, Sylvia prepares to leave. "There's a good cafe on the corner, should you require it," she flings over her shoulder, "but there's only seating for ten." On her way out she passes a band of beggars on the stairs who have somehow slipped past the concierge, and she tosses them a handful of coins hoping they will go away.

As soon as she is gone the china prince lies down on the bed and imagines he is in the encounter-tenor's office. "Think back to the first time you encountered the tenor," he thinks to himself.

And the woman, as soon as he ceased to dream about her, fell from the sky.

(The displacement of problems)

The encounter-tenor, after taking a phonecall from one of his little offspring, a B-flat pining in an orphanage in the Vatican City, turns his attention once more to the problem. "Ah, the problem," he says. "The difficulty of everything. There is always a problem."

China princes repeat, "The difficulty of everything. There is always a problem," over and over to themselves as if committing it to memory. They have a prodigious memory, as they told the dour troubadour way back when they wanted to be jongleurs and went in search of a *chansonnier*.

China princes lie on the couch and a spokesman tells the encounter-tenor they have a problem. "In our youth when we were single," he begins, "we once had the job of focus-puller on a short film on the subject of death. The film came out blurred but there was a particular woman who was of the utmost clarity."

"There, there," comments the encounter-tenor sympathetically.

"There's more," says the china prince.

"More!"

"Now we are experiencing fuzziness, the fuzziness of what has always been a very steady vision in seventeen different directions."

"It is making us motion sick," chips in another china prince.

"Yes, and we have great difficulty walking in a straight line across a room," says another. Now they are all clamouring to talk.

"As you can imagine, a fall is no small problem for a china prince."

"We have already lost our sackbuts. Where will it end?"

"My dear fellows!" exclaims the encounter-tenor. "I know exactly how you feel. I too have had many difficulties sent to try me. I was once a choirboy in the Vatican City, this in the days before castration had been dispensed with. I had a beautiful voice, and that voice . . ."

"Not only that," begins an excited china prince.

"No, not only that," says another, his voice rising, "we are, well, we are becoming increasingly dissatisfied with the life of an ornament. Aren't we?" The speaker appeals to the other china princes, who, having been shocked into silence, nod their heads in agreement. No one has dared say this before. After a few moments the china prince with the deepest voice says, "You said it."

"Well," says the encounter-tenor, sitting back. "That's quite a big one. It reminds me very much of my own predicament a few years ago. I was at the Vatican and I was becoming increasingly dissatisfied with my life there . . ."

"Attractive as it may sound," says the first spokesman slowly, "being suspended between one note and another does not make for stability."

"No."

"No."

"No."

"No," say the others.

"Quite frankly we are beginning to wish we had landed squarely on one note or another."

"Is that so?" inquires the encounter-tenor. "I sympathise entirely. I myself had just as traumatic an experience when I discovered the error of my ways in the Sistine Chapel. I was singing away one day when I realised I had put my trust in something that was actually myself. A watershed experience, I can tell you."

China princes nod.

"But I do believe that, like me, your problem can be solved. Just as I was able to leave my many children in the care of the Little Sisters of the Poor and get on with my own life, so you too — all of you — will soon find yourselves dropping your little foibles with ease. In fact, you have already demonstrated your ability to do this. Remember to build on what you've already accomplished."

"Oh yes," breathes an enthusiastic china prince, ". . . and which accomplishment was that?"

"Well, take the example of eccentricities," says the encounter-tenor, leaning back in his chair and putting his feet on the desk, his hands on the floor under it. From this position he reminds china princes, "You've told me that when you were a single china prince you adopted a host of peculiarities, such as reading a book in the street, wearing an evening suit on Thursdays to induce an eclipse of the sun, and reciting the rosary on a Friday. This was not normal behaviour — to wit, neuroses — but all were abandoned the moment you laid eyes on a woman. Or laid hands. Or anyway, laid, to put it bluntly," says the encounter-tenor, delicately crossing his palms. "I have no doubt that when you find another focus for your attention, seventeen points will narrow into one, different will become same again."

"And same different," think china princes.

"Don't worry," concludes the encounter-tenor, "you will become same."

At this, china princes get up from the couch, go to the window and look disconsolately down into the streetmap.

(The Selfish Giant, his winter)

There was a time
when she could count him on the fingers
of one hand
of the small
hands and feet.

(The long-lost Wolfgang returns from an ornament)

In 1791, his last year, perhaps with the knowledge that he had not long to go, Mozart turned his attention to God; this also in response to his becoming apprentice *Kapellmeister* in Vienna. It was expected he would take over the post when the ailing *Kapellmeister* died. But the present incumbent did not die, at least not immediately, and Mozart, for his part, did not live.

The Emperor Joseph had declared that Church music was becoming too ornamented and too heavily orchestrated for its original purpose, which was of course the glorification of God and the edification of the faithful. "Church music," announced Joseph, "would be more profound if it were plainer, and to the greater glory of God unadorned." *Vox populi* was *vox Dei*, the voice of the people, the voice of the divine, he said, adopting the tone of the Enlightenment.

Now it would not have been surprising if Mozart, long a lover of ornament, had regarded this as nonsense, but he entirely approved. He was after all a Mason, but it was not just that. He found himself being drawn more and more to

God, perhaps because of his approaching death. Accordingly, he composed the most formidable *Kyrie*, in a voice both poignant and direct, moving from one chord to another without his customary embellishment. In the same manner he wrote a motet for the feast of Corpus Christi, the greatest feast in all the Church, and this motet was *Ave, verum corpus*, in its turn the greatest motet in all the Church; and this motet was organum-like in style (like the stark parallel chords intended for a certain anonymous monk) apart from the fact that it was, of course, tonal and moved sideways like a crab through all the keys in Christendom (well, almost).

And with these works Mozart began to create what he saw as a new Church music, his particular vision of the Enlightenment, the style returning to the simplicity of plainsong, the spaces between notes left unornamented, unheard of, unheard. And he saw this new style forming the later period of his life.

A grey visitor, dressed in the way of Adrienne Monier, head to foot, called one day at the residence of Mozart. He spoke hissing through his teeth. "There will be a hundred Gulden for you in return for a requiem." A hundred Gulden was a princely sum in those days and Mozart was quite overcome. The grey visitor explained queasily, "The requiem is for an important guest, a guest to this world who was most concerned she should not outstay her welcome."

"She?" queried Mozart.

But the grey visitor would say nothing more, apart from to wheeze he would be back in a week, and to push ten Gulden into Mozart's hands.

Mozart, mistrusting the grey visitor but sorely in need of the hundred Gulden (particularly in view of his own failing health), took the coins to a flummoxed Constanze, and began at once to work on the requiem. It was to be a requiem, he said to himself sitting down at the keyboard, a chord falling from his plain linen cuff, in the style of the Enlightenment, without ornament, an Eighteenth Century organum of the most quelling simplicity.

He wrote in instalments, as arranged, and once a week the grey visitor visited to collect the finished pages. Each time he called he was more and more insistent that the requiem should be hurried. It would soon be required. "Our client has not long for this world," he buzzed. "She ails something terrible."

Mozart, strained by the pressure, became weaker and weaker and eventually he took to his sickbed. From there he wrote with a fever, a passion and the flickering of a flame. The more he wrote the more he flickered, and the more he became convinced he was writing the requiem of his own death.

Constanze, keeping a lonely vigil at the casement where she had once seen her husband disappear into the interval between one note and another — into the ornament of an aria or the slow movement of a piano concerto — now turned in disbelief to the man she had married ten years before. At first she barely recognised him, so changed had he become by his adventures between notes. Then she clasped him to her, crying, "Wolfgang! Wolfgang! Wolfgang was lost and now is found!"

And while Mozart hugged and kissed Constanze, he knew he belonged to the spaces between notes. Whereas once he had made this known with trills and turns and acciaccaturas, and the lacy ruffles that hung from his cuffs, now he went secretly into these places, not intending to return.

He wrote steadily, day and night, in a frenzy, sure he must finish the requiem in time for his death. Constanze appeared between phrases. "Could you take some broth, Wolfgang?" But Mozart now had little regard for his fading body. He cared only for the *Introit*, the *Kyrie*, the *Dies Irae*. His days were punctuated only by the accelerating knock of the grey visitor, pestering for completion.

Before he could finish the unadorned requiem, Mozart succumbed to his final illness. He died, penniless, tortured by the grey visitor whom he believed to be the Devil. Stonemasons fashioned an angel for his unmarked grave in the paupers' cemetery. No one could see it. It occurred between what is seen and what is seen.

Constanze, in widows' weeds, weeping, trying to comfort herself by dusting the ornaments of her late husband's hearing, accidentally dropped one, broke it, and was consumed then with real grief.

(A healthy respect for words)

When he sees from the balcony Sylvia coming along the street towards the *oubliette*, the single china prince, as if in a dream, pushes a tumble of the remaining china princes over the railing. A great crash is heard in the street below, the shattering of their limbs, their garments, their dear temples. Illuminations slough off their broken bodies and glide off in search of pages to rest on. The single china prince sheds six tears which fall next to Sylvia as she steps delicately over the rubble.

Having maintained the discreetness of a couple of hours' absence, a caution in word and deed, Sylvia ascends the stairs and revisits the *oubliette* to inquire after the novelette, and also after the china prince, his numerical status. "Well?" she demands as she stands in the middle of the room peeling off her gloves.

"With regard to the novelette," begins the china prince hesitantly, "it's difficult to say — there is always a difficulty, that is the nature of it. You must understand I've just come from a job on the roads, and here I am working on something that has no matter at all."

"And?" says Sylvia.

"Well, as for the little matter of the number of me, I am pleased to say, I am happy to say, extremely happy, that I am now a single man in every respect of the word."

A smile creeps over Sylvia's lips and she throws open the window recklessly.

"However," says the china prince, talking to the air above Sylvia's head rather than looking her in the eye, "there is another matter I should mention, and that is of the masculine and the feminine. Although I may appear as masculine as, say, your friend Joyce, there are parts of my make-up that on certain days are as feminine as you are (dear Sylvia). For instance, if a thought crosses my mind, it will more than likely pick its way delicately on high-heels, and if a feeling enters my heart it will probably be of the feminine persuasion. I am much given to feminine intuition and when it comes to modes, well, you would definitely not describe mine as phlegmatic." Here the china prince draws breath and steals a glimpse at Sylvia.

"What is the solution?" asks Sylvia simply of herself, and she puts her head in her hands for a moment to think. She thinks for a long moment, the longest the china prince has ever known. It is like a dream. Within it he considers his life on the Left Bank, that all his thoughts are ensconced here. Finally Sylvia reaches into her bag and brings out a pair of round spectacles which she plants firmly on the nose of the china prince, saying, "These will help you think along more masculine lines." They take root behind his ears. Then Sylvia takes off her coat and sits down in a chair, crossing her legs and lighting a cigarette.

(The Dissolution of the Monasteries)

And immediately the problem of clothes for the cold shrank to the size of a small mercy at her hands immersed in a hot wash. And the sleeves that had been maneouvered with such difficulty across a page, they were bundled up and sent by pigeon to St Vincent de Pawpaw.

The sudden caught breath of a windchime
was how they discovered
there was no wind
(and the chill factor had once bound
everything together) and then
how things fell apart!
A china scarf was found shattered
in the street outside
an apartment building

a kiss dying on a high ledge
and the twelve notes of the tempered scale
had all abandoned their
serial monogamy
for the perfect love of a Mode.

(What is the solution?)

A woman, *déshabillée*, is attempting to give alms to the poor on a streetmap of the Left Bank, which is where she has found herself quite by chance. For all she knows it could be the Right Bank. It depends which way you are facing. Left is Right, *Gauche est Droite*, wrong is right, and nothing is the way it is but the way it seems at the time.

When they see the state of her dishevelment, the beggars beg the woman not to part with her money. She, as much as they, looks like a vagrant. The woman has noticed the beggars' clothes are chipped and cracked, and that several of them have limbs missing or stuck on with a dried ooze of glue. But lowering her eyes she finds that indeed her own black evening dress is all askew and her possessions, such as they are, trail raggedly behind her. Nevertheless, she says to the beggars with a wave of the hand, "Oh, don't mind me, I've just returned from the Heavens."

"That's odd," say the beggars, "we've just returned from the Earths." And they laugh hysterically because of course there is only one Earth.

And the pair of them — the woman and the beggars — compare notes in the manner of tourists meeting at the top of the Matterhorn. The woman describes a day in the life of the night sky, speaking in a high, light voice: "I listened to the pure semi-quavers of counter-tenors. I observed a fancy dress party attended by nuns, heard a performance of chance music for motorway — this was the latest thing, the newest departure. There was much coming and going. I covered my ears against the clangour of all the modes of transport in order to hear everything. A troupe of jongleurs toured with their sackbuts and their dancing bears." The woman stops and sheds an unaccountable tear.

"Do go on," urge the beggars.

"I think I will stop here," says the woman, "although I could go on — there was much to be seen from the night sky. I felt like a soffit stopping visions in their tracks. Oh!" And more tears fall.

The beggars look from one to the other with their wall eyes (from recent damage), because an atom just turned over in its sleep.

Making a visible effort to pull herself together, the woman says loudly, "I sure could use a drink!" and drinks have not outlived their usefulness and she scouts about for a cafe. As it happens, she and the beggars are standing right outside one, this on the Left Bank. She is just about to go in when a woman unknown to her but known to the beggars and to us as Sylvia Ficta, appears in the doorway on her way out. As this new woman passes the tousled woman she presses into the palm of the cold gloveless hand, a franc.

"Thanks," says the woman, *dépeignée,* "a bunch." And she steps into the cafe.

The beggars, squashing their noses up against the window, say, "Uh oh", and this is their last gasp before crumbling into a pile of rubble.

(and of the convents)

Pawpaw Claire!
Little Sisters of the Pawpaw!
The pawpaw will always be with us!
The poet will always be with us!
The poetry of the Masses!
The Ordinary of the Mass and the Proper of the Mass!
The displacement of the Mass!
The music of the Mass and wind of the Mass!
Choirs of angels!
The fall of the Angels!
The way atoms have fallen!
What is the matter? How
cold it is!

(~~Five~~ Four beats in Arthur Rubinstein)

He is Russian but the Passions
of Bach and the Requiems of

Mozart are what move him
ornaments dusted between notes

by a woman who leaves things
just as she found them, the webby

passages of accidentals and
the way atoms fell once, all

within the Common Time grazings
of a stave. He came from the

Steppes, snow, but lent an ear
to the West, a leading note landing

with a flight of Jews among the
tenements and music schools of

New York, New York.
                       Never departing

the many articles of his winter
summers among the motions of a

bus travelling the streets at
right and left angles, incidents

in 4/4 time en route including
Mozart by rote among the contents

of his heart: Rubinstein finds
he cannot commit the deeds of Bartók

to memory, five beats together
impudent beyond measure, he says.

(Word indeed)

Presently Hildegard discovered that there were more ways than one of making flesh word. This was the history: She had once been blinded by the light of scholars and theologians, in their presence had been made blind to visions, and so she had invented visions. Knowing became wondering.

Now one day as she scribbled down furiously the adventures appearing on the ceiling of her cell — tossing the pages onto the floor to be recovered by a monk at her elbow who illuminated with star lighting her texts; and the texts to be copied by the monk, Volmar, and thence to be sent to go before the wonderment of the Pope of the day who was Pope Eugenius III — she found that for a moment, once again, her ceiling drew a complete blank, apart from the centuries-old cracks in the palm of its hand. This time Hildegard did not miss a beat. She continued to babble and the artist continued to draw and Volmar continued to write; but where were these visions coming from? For the second time in her life, Hildegard considered the possibility that a vision could be born of her own head, of the planting of seeds there, and still have a miraculous reflection throughout Christendom. And that is exactly what happened.

Hildegard of *The Bright Cloud and the Shadow*, and of the Garment Embroidered with Tears, and of the fields of sleeves sliding across pages, and of the conception of all weeping, now believed that a vision did not exist until someone had seen it, and that nothing was an idea until someone had thought it; and she had seen many things in her life and they were now visions, and she had thought many things in her life and they were now ideas. For instance, the principle of the theology of the feminine: that woman is a creator as God is a creator, of the word made flesh; and therefore woman, clasping a baby to her breast, was more in the image of God than was man, who had cast out this baby from his loins. This was not an idea until

Hildegard had thought of it, but once she had thought of it, then it was an idea.

And once an idea exists it cannot be destroyed. It is a possession of the possessed.

And so it was with the idea of Hildegard had had with regard to convents: that she would like a new one to be built to cope with the swelling numbers of postulants attracted to the order by the fame of her visionary powers. Hildegard believed the new convent should be at Rupertsburg, opposite Bingen am Rhein, because Rupertsburg had appeared to her in a vision, there was no mistaking it was Rupertsburg. She foresaw Rupertsburg as a retreat, and a place where she would have absolute dominion. On this subject she had entreated Kuno, Abbot of St Disibod's, and Heinrich, Archbishop of Mainz. Now she petitioned them once again, but again to no avail.

Thus thwarted, Hildegard retired to her bed with the most terrible illness — an ague, a paralysis in her limbs, the partial stoppage of her heart (and of her soul, almost). She cried, "I am at death's door!"

And it was the first time anyone had put it quite like that, and the phrase was repeated through the abbey, and the monks and nuns came running from all directions, whispering to each other, "Hildegard is at death's door!" And the squeaky opening of death's door echoed all through Christendom.

When Pope Eugenius III got wind of it, a dove hovering at his ear, he asked quite simply, "Why is Hildegard at this *'death's door'*?" The message was relayed back through all the abbeys of Europe, linked by the telepathic company of flocks of doves — "*Why* is Hildegard at death's door?"

Hildegard, lying in her bed, her flesh all atremble, and gazing up at the ceiling of her cell, replied, "Because I see, and it is not done."

Doves carrying this message back to the Pope said to each other, "It shall be done, you mark my words."

And it was done.

And immediately Hildegard made a miraculous recovery, and it was another miracle, and as work began on the new convent at Rupertsburg, she rose up from her sickbed and, together with her band of nuns, packed her bags.

And that is how the flesh of Hildegard was made word.

(Loved, Left Bank)

His thoughts are exactly the size of a little table in a cafe on a street corner near the Seine. If someone comes to join him at the table, his thoughts must move over like shopping bags being lifted from seats, cups cleared away, and crumbs collected from vinyl with a damp cloth. As soon as the company is gone the china prince monopolises all the chairs again, and the entire table. He pins his thoughts to the chequered tablecloth. They like a table just this size, his thoughts, and always on the Left Bank. A table contains a certain amount of his life; there is no other way for his life to be contained. Imagine a life without afternoons — where would it go? For the china prince it is the same with a particular table and thoughts, and that is why he has come to the Left Bank to have them.

Theoretically, in the cafe on the Left Bank, at this very table, one could think about anything one liked. That is the thinking on these matters. But the actuality of it is for the china prince, his thinking is dictated by things outside him, pulled this way and that by everything in the universe apart from his thoughts. When the wind blows furiously his thoughts are in accordance; a music likewise affects him; when it rains his thoughts are rained upon; when a woman a long way off dreams an ordinary dream, so his dreaming becomes ordinary. This is the way it has always been, it's just that he did not expect such a thing on the Left Bank, no. He is very sad. Why is there such sadness? he wonders, ordering a coffee.

(Eureka, the displacement of seas)

China prince visiting the encounter-tenor once more finds a note pinned to his door to the effect that the encounter-tenor has married an alto clef and has gone off on honeymoon. China prince shrugs his shoulders and shambles back to the *oubliette* where nothing awaits him but his novelette. "It is natural to grieve for the loss of many of me," he says over and over to comfort himself. He wades through Sylvia's clothes and make-up and flings himself on the bed. Sylvia appears from the bathroom.

"What's the matter now?" she asks.

(The earthly passion of Beethoven)

One day, following a deafening applause, he realised suddenly his hearing had left him. Immediately he flew into a rage (as was his wont at even the slightest provocation), mouthing, "This is what an audience has done to me!" He believed the demands for kettle drums, trombones, large scale orchestras, had broken up his ménage à trois.

Taking out his anger on the thing dearest to him, he seized a saw, rushed to the piano and severed the legs from her. (And several women who had once contemplated marriage with Beethoven breathed a collective sigh of relief from their various kitchens in the vicinity of Bonn.) Then Beethoven sat cross-legged, himself de-legged, in front of his once-beloved keyboard and pounded out the angriest noise anyone had ever laid ears on. His rage was unprecedented, unheard of and, for a long time, unheard. This suited Beethoven down to the ground, who believed an audience had robbed him of his performance. And the vibrations from the strings of the piano ran along the floorboards as if the floorboards were fuse, until they found what they were looking for — the great man himself. And they leapt upwards into Beethoven's body, and there they exploded with enormous resonance.

For if he could not hear, by God he would feel! Or he would taste, or he would smell, he vowed, licking the piano all over and inhaling the cold scent of her keys. Or he would see. Beethoven, fuming and foaming, saw what is not heard.

(Espalier)

A sameness
brought them
together

a difference
entwined them, a

sameness
drove them
apart.

(A familiar breed of contempt)

In a cafe she has entered to escape, momentarily, the streetmap, the woman finds there is but one seat free and it is at a table already occupied by a man and his thoughts, the warp and the woof of them and the red and the white of them, and there are so many thoughts they cover the entire table and hang over the sides in crisp points. When she sits down at the table the edges of the thoughts lie in the woman's lap.

She looks away nervously. A woman recently returned from the night sky is, after all, a little different from the usual clientele. The waiter gives her a sidelong glance, takes note of the state of her dress and decides to let her sit a while to show who's boss. However, the customers in the cafe nod politely and she nods back. Then she looks from beneath lowered eyelids at the man sitting opposite and observes that he is writing furiously on paper serviettes as if taking dictation from the thoughts on the table. His left hand is held aloft as if to say, "*Attend*, I've just had a thought!" This continues for a long moment. A long moment is not very different from a short one, from the outside, but from the inside, as in dreams, it can take as long as it would to paint the Sistine ceiling on the curve of an eyelid.

Presently the waiter throws a paper serviette folded into a dart at the woman and saunters over to take her order. Her order is very long because she hasn't eaten for a good while. The waiter, licking his pencil, scribbles it all down on his pad and when she has finished he tears off the sheet with a perfectly executed glissando. "And a *demitasse*," says the woman. The waiter clicks his tongue, *spiccato*, and starts on another sheet of paper. When he has torn off this second sheet, with slightly less of a flourish, the woman adds, "And coffee to follow."

At the sound of her voice (he had not noticed her physical presence), the man opposite, disturbed in his thought-making, looks up and straightaway there is the merest flicker of recognition between them. She thinks, "Could it be?" And he thinks, "No, it could not." There is something about people dressed for the streetmap that gives them a sameness.

"This table is where I always come to think," says the man.

"I beg your pardon?" asks the woman.

With the air of the long-suffering the man begins again. "I *think* here, you know, idea, lightbulb, hmm? I'm sorry but you'll have to find another place to sit."

The woman spreads her hands in a gesture encompassing the cafe as if to say, Look, this is the only spare seat!

The other patrons, on cue, sing a little chorus in her favour — *Yes, Carmen has the only remaining seat in the cafe.*

At this, the man takes a large sigh, recrosses his legs, half turns away from her and, with his left hand now held up over his brow as a visor against her glare, continues his work — not before muttering, "But don't expect any small-talk. I have serious thinking to do."

"Of course," says the woman, and at that moment her order arrives.

The woman, engaged in the systematic devouring of delicacies, notices that although the man tries hard not to appear interested, he can hardly keep his eyes off them. She offers him, tentatively, a bite of her éclair — "Here" —

but at that particular moment he is too deep in thought to hear.

When she comes to the last sip of a pawpaw smoothie, the woman makes a little gurgle with her straw. The man opposite gives her a dark look from under his brow and rearranges his limbs, causing a stray thought to follow its own whimsical path to the floor. The man makes a grab for it but the woman, trying to be helpful, also possibly a little curious, bends to pick it up as well. Their heads meet on the way down, and again on the way up. There are two high-pitched reports. The woman peers closely and sees that the man winces in pain and that he now has two faint cracks in his skull. His skull is made of china.

At this realisation she gasps and clutches the thought more tightly in the ungloved hand that drips from her frayed sleeve. The man extends his china hand for the thought but the woman is momentarily mesmerised. She looks into his eyes and sees the rapid movement of dreams rushing across the surface of a dome, and choirs raise their voices towards this ceiling in the most rapturous rendition of passion, and it is a moment of deja vu, and therefore also of this moment.

And he, looking into the eyes of the woman, is reminded most painfully that they set out to breed love and instead bred contempt.

So far the woman has not even glanced at the thought in her hand, but now she does so and she reads, *The Council of Magic Realists, Their Used Carpets, Salesmen, and What is Swept Under Them*, and then she mouths these words without looking at the text, knowing them, knowing everything, as this is a thought that has already befallen her. Then she asks crisply, "Where did you get *this*?"

The man, leaping up from the table and displacing the Mass of his own weight, replies, "I found it."

The woman gets to her feet and says firmly, "I found it." To which the man replies with an air of pity, "Sorry, but *I* found it." Whereupon she repeats at a high pitch, "I found it!" and he screams at the top of his voice, *"I found it! I found it!"*

The other customers in the cafe begin to look alarmed and the waiter strolls over to the deal with the disturbance. "Now then, we'll have none of this," he says, in French.

But the man and the woman, unheeding, continue with their kerfuffle. She removes a pin deftly from a thought skewered to a red check, and then another, and another, and these loosened thoughts flutter about the cafe. At the fourth dislodgement the man, who has been flapping ineffectually after them, bellows and tries to stop the woman, making a grab for her hand. In the process her hand closes on the pin and she pricks her finger, gives a yelp and puts her finger immediately to this yelp where it leaves her mouth, as if to staunch it. She looks accusingly at the man, and angels trickle down her chin.

The waiter, concerned for his trade, grasps the subject of the altercation, the tablecloth, whips it cleanly out from under the dirty crockery (which remains standing), bundles it up and throws it out the window. Then he hurls the man and the woman out onto the streetmap.

Outside, the woman asks the man, "Should we have tipped?" to which the man makes a hundred outlandish replies.

(The reversal of everything, even a mode)

And an earthquake rents the Earth asunder; and birds fly up screeching from the tremblings of their nests; and animals, trumpeting and yowling, run for their lives; and the wind whips itself into a tremendous flurry, making notes from tunnels like the pipes of an organ; and comets go haywire, travelling all journeys between Heaven and Earth in quick succession; and every tree blooms, bears fruit, sheds its leaves, blooms again, all in the space of a light year; and the Northern Lights are extinguished never to be lit again; and light becomes dark; and the Southern Hemisphere discovers the Northern, quite by accident, blown onto the Northern Seaboard; and spiralling bathwater ascends again to the bath; and hammocks that once hung peacefully now billow upwards and the bodies underneath cling to these pods; and human nature is turned on its head; and a newspaper article says there is a flaw in the theory of relativity only its precise whereabouts has not been discovered yet; and Renaissance men forget everything they have ever known; and possessed thoughts are exorcised by priests swinging incense; and the incense flees madly from nostrils; and the physics of music moves backwards leaving the good behaviour of the tempered scale, passing through the idiosyncracies of modes and arriving at the generic moods and elements; and all notes are immediately recalled to where they came from, a stampede towards the apertures of flutes, strings quaking with the wildness of homing birds; and the love-struck sinews of pianos, once eloping in twos and threes, now petition the Pope for annulments and come home to their mothers; and every piano in every living-room resounds with this; and every living creature in every living-room becomes moribund; and every singer finds their diaphragm suddenly bursting with the long-lost strains of every aria they have ever sung; and there is such cacophany that people come rushing out of their houses into the streets, and the houses become passages between, and the streets dwelling places, and streetmaps redundant; and ornaments fall from shadow boxes, throwing their structure into a state of flux; and the bones of brontasauri, fleshed, burst through the revolving doors of museums in search of water; and fur cups and saucers return to the wild; and winter becomes summer; and everything made of china turns to flesh; and a woman dealing her trump card, a blow to a man, and expecting him to shatter, sees instead he stays intact, and he winces in pain, and this is the first pain she has ever seen, and she touches gently his forehead, and it is not cold, it is tepid; and Rubinstein, hearing the faint murmurings of a summer storm from his place on the production line at the factory, looks heavenwards and exclaims, "Ah, a thunderous applause!"

And when the Ficta is about to fall with a splash into the Seine, which has changed direction and so now they are on the Rive Gauche, she says, "What do you expect — normal behaviour? Oh, my china prince, what have we done!"

And he says, "It is not necessary to live it." And he cries, and he cries.

(A tear-shaped globe to show they have been there)

What will he bring her
from the hanging gardens

he has dangled in during
the winter of his babbling

brook? A tree trained in
symmetry, physics and the flight-

paths of birds
his wonderings and the mysteries

of the rosary, a cult
figurine fashioned in blessed

plaster by a series of monks
all cast in the same mold

(the difference between them)?
A grape press extracts perfect

pitches in the likeness of Jesus
Christ, of neumes and of jugs

of pure water changed by an
alchemist into the *Young Person's*

Guide to the Orchestra.
Oh the avenues of these notes

are stopped up with soffits
preventing evaporation or Middle Cs

leaving this world prematurely —
instead condensed. Like Rubinstein

taking a bus from Auckland to
South Auckland, an assumption

of gracenotes he has merely
imagined so they won't leave

his head. Were a prince to keep
a miniature score (an ornament)

of these moments he would find
they were very real.

There was always
a problem with the tick of a clock,

when it was also hers.
As a gift she would like

a souvenir of the world, a small
article of the difficulty of it

(The Gift of Tears).

(Their complete Pope Urban XVII)

When the raffle is drawn it is won, of course, by the Lands. The prize is the jar of pedestrians. The Lands take the jar home and tip its contents out on the floor of their two-bedroom flat and under the light of the electric bulb they begin to count, just to make sure. The figure, when they arrive at it, solves a mystery. Now there is no more wondering. They have left the Dark Ages behind. Now there are as many pedestrians in the flat as Goths sacked Rome, and the Lands are completely urbanised.

"But what shall we do with the pedestrians?" asks the youngest Land.

The other Lands look at him. That is the only question. The family sit round in the long evenings pondering it. They have always been Catholic, but now a mystery is a decade, every last minute of it.

(The Council of Magic Carpets and What is Swept under Them)

Pope John XXIII — the man who called together the bishops and cardinals of the Catholic Church for the Second Vatican Council between 1962 and 1965 — was already an old man, no more than a concierge, a doorman who slept in a little room at the bottom of the stairs. He vetted who came in and who went out, he sorted the mail, he took out the rubbish, he swept away the particles of dust that sloughed off the bodies of the clergy.

*("Remember man that thou art
is!")*

Now this Caretaker Pope swept so furiously, shook out his duster with such passion, that all the elements of the universe were disturbed, and people heard a great music blowing through the Church, and some said, "He has opened the window and let in the breeze," and others said, "He has opened up the whole roof and everything is being sucked up into the sky — the music of the Church and the liturgy of the Church, all the old *poetry*, and the sacraments and the teachings and traditions of the Church" — anything, in fact, that was lighter than air. And a wind had once held all matter together, and now it was blowing all that mattered apart.

And monks and nuns began dressing differently, as the person in the street, in a multifarious range of styles and colours. But the paradox is, when people try to be different they are the same, and when they are the same they are

How cold it is! But it is almost Spring

p. 134
XXXVI

Tromba Marina

different. And the old school, wanting still the old poetry of the Mass, said, *"La Seine!"* And the new school said, *"La différence."* And this was the beginning of an even greater schism in the Church.

Into which one day everything will fall.

The concern of the Council of Magic Realists, glissing along on their mode of transport, was not how many people can dance on the head of a pin (that could now be worked out in a laboratory) but why are the angels there. "And indeed, why are the pins there?" the Caretaker Pope asked of his bishops.

When the old school said, "How can this nonsense be stopped?", the Caretaker Pope answered, "It cannot."

(Litotes)

An encounter-tenor has not been without love. He is back from his honeymoon on the high seas. On Monday morning he is surprised to find his former client, the china prince, in his office. "What can I do for you?" he asks, summoning the limited attention span of the recently honeymooned.

The prince wanders over to the window and looks down into the street, where street-sweepers are shovelling a collection of shards into a refuse truck. "There is a little matter I would like to address," he says.

"But I thought you were cured," says the encounter-tenor.

"Oh, make no mistake," says the prince proudly, "I've got rid of my alter egos."

"All of them?" inquires the encounter-tenor tentatively.

"All of them," replies the prince, and the encounter-tenor shifts uneasily in his chair.

"Bar one," adds the prince.

"Which one might that be?" asks the encounter-tenor, pressing the tips of his toes together to form a perfect pyramid.

The prince replies that it is the one that was not china, and therefore could not be broken along with the others.

"You didn't tell me about this one," says the encounter-tenor, wounded.

"It was never necessary," replies the prince. "This ego could speak for itself."

And so he continues, telling the encounter-tenor that as he, the encounter-tenor, predicted, his china forms dropped away, just like that — and he snaps his fingers. Now that he has discarded the china, his body is made of a substance both soft and strong, neither hot nor cold, breakable but able to be mended. His sleeves are now silk, and his coat and hat, which once were unbending, now blow about in the wind. And a music howls from the north-west, but it is a warm music. It is no longer winter. It is no longer than the length of a winter coat.

"This is all to the good," says the encounter-tenor. "However, I have no doubt that one day you will be able to confront the china of your youth once again. Time heals all. I myself once made a living by picking up odd jobs as an itinerant vocalist in Renaissance consorts. Then I married — not before obtaining an annulment from my marriage to the Catholic Church on grounds of unfaithfulness; I had lost my faith. Now that I am married, we are involved in the complicated legal proceedings of adopting back my children, the fruit of my voice, whom I left behind in the Vatican orphanages."

The prince is of the opinion that his china sleeves, his china hat and coat, etc. have left him never to return, but he refrains from arguing with the encounter-tenor. Instead he says, "Look, I have no sackbut," and spreads the palms of his hands to display their emptiness. "So I can't be a jongleur any more. It was once my greatest desire to be a whole troupe of jongleurs, but now I am none at all, even myself is not one. It's strange but wanting to be jongleurs has passed, and being jongleurs has passed."

"All things must pass," says the encounter-tenor.

"I knew you were going to say that," says the prince.

The encounter-tenor clears his throat. "No longer a vagabond — but still a prince?" he asks, thinly disguising his apprehension by rocking to and fro in his chair. His concern is that the prince will have nothing left if all his idiosyncracies leave him; that he will find, after the session, the skin of a young man in a pool on the floor of his office, like hastily discarded clothing. Also he worries where these foibles will go. Where do they go? The encounter-tenor may find himself responsible for stray eccentricities at large in the world, and be sued for malpractice. The trials and tribulations of an encounter-tenor's life! the encounter-tenor laments to himself. Oh, the difficulty of everything! There is always a problem. "But still a prince?" he repeats aloud.

The prince hesitates.

The encounter-tenor bursts into tears. "I'm sorry," he wails, reaching for the tissues he has strategically placed for the use of his clients when recalling the trauma of their childhoods. But there have been more traumatic childhoods than tissues, and the empty box has a dull resonance.

"There, there," croons the prince, taking the encounter-tenor's feet in his hands and endeavouring to comfort him — but to no avail. "You certainly do have the gift of tears!" he tries, but this does no good either. The prince sighs and decides to proceed with the session regardless. It is costing him a lot of money. Thankfully the encounter-tenor makes a visible effort to pull himself together, coming out in what he believes to be a cup and saucer, if he is lucky, a bunch of knots, if he is not.

"It is the prince I would like to consider," confides the prince to the snivelling encounter-tenor. "Sometimes I feel as if the prince is my alter ego and I myself am someone entirely different — the subject of the sentences instead of the speaker, the audience instead of the performer, one who wonders rather than one who knows."

"That's too bad," says the encounter-tenor, dabbing his eyes on a map of the world. "You want to be careful you don't lose your ego altogether."

"But encounter-tenor, what if I did?" cries the prince. "What if I *did* abandon my ego? Perhaps that is what I must do . . ."

The encounter-tenor sniffs. "I can give you advice," he says briskly, "but I can't force you to take it. Neither can I be expected to deal with the consequences if you decide to go your own way."

The prince thinks this is a bit harsh, especially seeing he has just comforted the encounter-tenor, but he says, "With all due respect, encounter-tenor, I may not have any choice."

The encounter-tenor's next piece of advice to the prince is for him to settle his account with the receptionist on his way out. "Which by this time," says the encounter-tenor with relish, "will be a princely sum."

Truer words were never spoken. The prince spends everything in the encounter-tenor's office. He empties the pockets of his sumptuous trousers, hands over the last gold piece. He is no longer a prince.

(The awoken by a clock dusting its hands)

A first kiss to enter
sleep, the sleep made

entirely of dream:
a finger pricked

for a hundred years
of wakefulness?

(Hildegard disregarding the theologians)

Arriving at Rupertsburg, Hildegard discovered to her surprise that it was spring; and she went straightaway outside to a secluded arbour containing the warmest wall to be found in the garden, and she weeded until she revealed an espalier growing there. And the tree bore the blossoms of spring. And postulants blew all over the garden in their white habits like the accoutrements of spring.

As she worked, weeding, Hildegard recalled the time when winter first set in. She was eight years old, free as a bird, the youngest child left to her own devices in the hot dry summers of Disibodenberg. Though she had been schooled for the cloister since the age of five, she was unprepared for the reality of it. She kissed her parents goodbye, and her nine brothers and sisters. She knew she would be joining Jutta, the anchoress, who had been living an eremetical life for a number of years. A large and breathless crowd had gathered for the ceremony — the Archbishop officiating — at the small opening in the almost-sealed room. There was just enough room in the stone wall for Hildegard to walk through. She did so. The faithful sent up sighs, petitions and acts of contrition towards Heaven as she went.

Hildegard was confined! She drew breath to scream — No! No! — but did not protest. To be walled up was considered an honour. Since the age of five Hildegard had been told she was specially chosen. Had not her soul arrived on this earth in the auspicious body of the tenth child? She turned back towards the opening in the wall, saw a last glimpse of her family just as a monk cemented the last stone in place. That was the way her mother remembered her, the diminutive child in the black habit, her tenth, half turned towards the decreasing light. When the daylight had gone, Hildegard turned to the anchoress, whose cadaverous face reflected the beams of a lamp, and of her inner being.

From then on there was winter, winter, winter and winter. "Do you think the monastery garden belongs to the Selfish Giant?" Hildegard asked Jutta one day. Jutta said this was a profane thing, and Hildegard replied, "No, it is but an allegory." But although it was always winter, Hildegard harboured some small spring and she tended it where it resided against the grey ceiling of the cell. And she dwelt in this spring more and more, until one day Jutta said peevishly to a visiting monk (in fact they were not entirely confined), "She may as well live perpetually in spring like the birds that flock above the monastery." In this way Hildegard tells you how it is.

As the weeding saint mused she looked up and saw suddenly, making her catch her breath, the jongleur who had once visited her cell. He appeared like a vision in front of the wall; there was nowhere he could have come from but the wall. And Hildegard remembers him as a funny boy who had the idea he must live his novelette, and she smiles to herself, and she calls to him, "Jongleur! Jongleur! How goes it?" And the jongleur looks up from his worried frown, and Hildegard sees he is with a woman and they have both just stepped from the warm wall where they have been entwined. They are shaking out their legs in unaccustomed freedom, and have their hands extended as if to survey their palms.

"The saint!" murmurs the man, and at the sound of his voice the woman looks up too and sees a diminutive nun, shrouded from head to toe in a rough habit.

"My dear jongleurs! How you have changed!" exclaims Hildegard. "Tell me, what is it that is different?" Here Hildegard affectionately lifts a lock of his hair and peers underneath as if to find more jongleurs.

"I am single now," he replies.

Hildegard drops the lock of hair. "Single?" she asks. They both look at the woman and laugh.

"Why don't you introduce your friend?"

"Oh!" blurts the man. "She is the woman."

Hildegard and the woman smile at each other, the smile of the shared knowledge of the man.

"Do sit down," invites Hildegard.

They sit on tree stumps and at that moment a flock of postulants arrives with rice cakes and herb tea.

"You must give us a tune, jongleur," says Hildegard presently. "We would like to be entertained in our new convent. You know, there are only women here. It is really quite radical. The postulants are like Aeolian harps hung in a tree and strummed by the wind."

The man and the woman exchange glances, remembering.

"But Saint, as you see, I am no longer a jongleur," says the man.

"Not a jongleur? Oh my vagabond prince! What has become of you? Do you not know that the symphony stands for the spirit? That through the power of hearing, God reveals the hidden mysteries?"

The man shrugs and smiles shyly, liking the attention Hildegard showers upon him. Like many religious she treats all non-religious like children, believing them to be so in the eyes of God.

"Nor a prince," he adds presently.

"You used to be such a delicate, shiny collection of ornaments! How I admired your gold tips when you came that day to my cell."

"Saint . . ." protests the man, his soft face drooping with a sudden sadness.

"And your writing," says Hildegard quickly. "How is the novelette coming along? Remember you used to think you had to live it?" Here Hildegard giggles behind her hand, and throws a merry look of collusion in the direction of the woman.

"It's going very well," says the woman in a clear voice.

"Is it now?" Hildegard swivels round on her tree stump to face her. "Are you a writer too?"

"No," the woman hedges. "Once I set out to write about him" — she jerks her head at the man in a familiar way, not without affection — "but I ended up writing of myself. It's difficult to keep the self out of it, so I found."

"Oh I do agree," says Hildegard sipping her tea. "I have the same problem with my visions. Some days I am convinced everything I imagine is a projection of myself. This is just between you and me, mind."

"Yes, yes, of course," hastens the woman, pleased at this intimacy. "Just between these four walls."

And all three of them look about them at the garden. Blossoms are breaking on the boughs of the apple trees.

"I think, Saint, the matter might be between you and *me*," the man says to Hildegard with emphasis, casting a sidelong glance at the woman, "for I am the one who wrote the novelette."

The woman tightens her lips as if to say she's not going to argue in public; dirty laundry, etc. She allows, "We'll see," to escape her lips, like a valve opening and shutting, and lets that suffice. But "we'll see" has such force behind it, it travels all the way to the clouds and back again, and echoes about the garden. A few pale postulants drift past to see what the matter is.

Hildegard replaces her cup on its saucer and looks from the woman to the man. Then she clasps her hands and looks up into the sky. A flock of birds is passing overhead. "Once I looked up into the sky," says Hildegard, "and saw the miraculous reflection of my wishes. I knew all I needed to do was watch them and they would entertain me." She gets up from her stump and twirls about on the grass, a girl again. "Oh how good it is to be at Bingen! I am, after all, Hildegard of Bingen."

Now the woman leaps to her feet as well. Her black tatters float about her as she dances.

"And tell me," asks Hildegard as they wave their arms in formation, "why are *you* here? I know why *he's* here." She giggles.

The woman thinks for a minute and then says soberly, "A kiss to enter sleep, the sleep made entirely of dream."

"Why, that sounds like something that happened to one of our young postulants," says Hildegard. "Elisabeth. She came to us after that."

"We found ourselves in the same dream. There was such happiness, but then . . . unhappiness."

The man looks at the woman darkly. "One morning I left," he tells Hildegard. "It was an ordinary dream and, as you know, Saint, I had a yen to be jongleurs."

"But Saint," says the woman, "he did not leave! Or rather, I went too — oh, I don't know!" Here the woman hurls herself onto the grass. By and by she says softly, "We set out to love."

"Of course you did," soothes Hildegard, in her adult-to-child tone. "You know, I'll tell you something, it was because of my aloneness that I saw the ceiling. Eight years old! I was so so alone."

The man pours more tea.

"Oh!" says the woman, sitting up and casting her arms in the air once more. She is quite carried away with the sadness of dreams and of ceilings.

The postulants have gathered behind a bush to watch. They are like an afternoon's washing, their expressions like new sheets.

"Indeed I had a tutor, Jutta — but my dears, she was no company for a child. Had I had a girl my own age to whisper with and tell secrets to at night, I doubt I would have looked to the ceiling to comfort me."

"Ah, I know exactly what you mean," says the woman, "If I had had company I would not have intended the *Ficta*."

The man raises his eyebrows in astonishment. "Well I'm staggered," he says.

"Pairs are the very devil!" curses the woman.

Hildegard chuckles and sits down on the stump. "Well, I don't know about that. But certainly it's not possible for two to be party to the same enlightenment. Which brings us back to the problem of the *Ficta*. What's to be done?"

"I have an idea," says the man, showing his teeth and holding one finger aloft, "and that is to divide it in half."

"Oh yes, down the middle, so it comes out like a Michelin guide," says the woman.

"No, no, my dears," says Hildegard. "That wouldn't do at all. Haven't you read of Solomon and the baby?"

"Well, what is the solution?" asks the man solemnly.

"The solution?" sighs Hildegard. "The solution is that one of you must go."

"Go?"

"Go. Leave the *Ficta*. The *Ficta* must be left."

Suddenly everything stops. The woman stops her dance. The man pauses with his cup halfway to his lips. They look at each other and look away again. The postulants hold their breath.

The man and woman nod. They know it is true, have perhaps always known it, although there was no knowing.

"Who must go? How are we to decide?" asks the woman.

"It depends on who has written the *Ficta*," says the man, "which is of course I."

"I have written it!" cries the woman.

"It is not a matter of who has written it, or even who has thought it . . ." says Hildegard.

"I thought it!" cry the man and the woman simultaneously.

Hildegard sighs. Her sigh is not one of annoyance but of pause, as a dove beats its wings to remain stationary in the air. ". . . but who is true to it, who lets it go its own way without hindering it. In short, who loves it."

Bells ring in the distance. The postulants sail off in the direction of the convent.

"One of you must bow out gracefully," says Hildegard, "even if it is the author. I myself leave my visions to be collected by the Church. They will always be my visions, because I have thought them, though the Church guards them jealously."

"I have had everything taken from me, and I'm not giving up the *Ficta*!" cries the man and glares defiantly at the woman.

"If you love the *Ficta*," repeats Hildegard, "you will be able to let it go."

"Okay," says the woman.

"What?" retorts the man.

"Okay, you can have it."

The man folds his arms. "Oh. All right then," he says.

"You can have it," repeats the woman.

The postulants have gone into the chapel and the party in the garden can hear them intoning *None*. The man and the woman bend their ears to listen. As she gets up to go in, Hildegard looks from one to the other and a tiny furrow creases her brow because she does not for one moment believe the woman.

(The moment of his greatest reality repeats itself)

He is on a bus travelling from Auckland to South Auckland, flicking over, with furious intent, the pages of the miniature score of a piano concerto propped up on the stand provided. He is trying to imagine the sound of seventeen instruments played simultaneously, but today his mind is racing in all directions. When he comes to a half-cadence, like a comma, he looks up and notices that Rubinstein has temporarily abandoned his piano score. It lies in his lap like a map and his hands, spare and muscular from many trips to and from the factory, also lie motionless. His attention is caught by the gaze of the man opposite.

Arthur Rubinstein smiles apologetically, feeling a little foolish. "Ah, I was miles away!" he says. Then he looks around the bus at the other musicians, most of whom are very much his junior. He says to the man with an air of conspiracy, "Some of these bright young players are learning Bartók off-by-heart — miles of him! I could never do that, not in ten years."

"But surely," ventures the other, "a man like yourself, a foreman..."

"No," says Rubinstein. "Never anything with so many accidentals. I can memorise classical music with no trouble. In the time it takes to travel from Auckland to South Auckland I can commit an entire Mozart sonata to memory, and go home in the evening and play it to my wife. But not this music with so many extra sharps and flats, and five beats to boot."

The younger man looks around him at the other passengers in the bus, all busily studying the contents of their hearts notated on small pages, and he sees them, in a revelation, as real people. This is the moment of his greatest reality.

(A blind bit of difference)

On the banks of their eyelids
a man and a woman, *distraits*

the way it has fallen
the *Ficta* into the river

Vive la Seine! she cries *(la différence)*.

(A dour troubadour retrieves his *chansonnier*)

An upright man, not grand but nevertheless the master of a respectable stable of jongleurs, said to his wife as they travelled into Paris, "That's the last time I trust a rich kid with a songbook."

"My dear," she said gently, touching his fat arm to soothe his anger. She had had nine years of this.

But it was jealousy he felt more than anger — the troubadour, that is, of his apprentice.

In the nine long years since the jongleur in question had first come to see him — knocked on his door, blown into a sackbut, and begged to become apprentice to his sorcery — the dour troubadour had heard frequent reports of the havoc wreaked on his absent *chansonnier*. He had handed over this document in good faith, expecting its contents to be aired in castles and monasteries for good returns; a jongleur was a travelling salesman for the wares of the troubadour. It was said, however, that in this case elaborate embroideries were being added in the performance, so much so that the original *chansonnier* had long been forgotten. This was for the entertainment of others, yes, but more so, it seemed, for the entertainment of the jongleur himself.

The dour troubadour had heard these entertainments only by repute, apart from once hearing a glimpse through the grille in a monastery wall. Those few notes were remarkable, but it was more what came inbetween the notes that impressed: the ornaments. For a good while the dour troubadour would rush to a town at a moment's notice if he got word that the jongleur had performed in its vicinity. But he couldn't keep that up. He had other, well-behaved jongleurs to attend to, and anyway the jongleur would always have departed, leaving only reports of his astonishing repertoire. It was said the contents of the *chansonnier* were inspired from above. The dour troubadour knew this not to be so, but secretly hankered to hear the jongleur for himself and discover his trick. Never had the troubadour received such praise for his songs, which for many years had been spread far and wide by his apprentices. The dour troubadour, not one to give praise himself, could not but admire his errant jongleur; his elusiveness, his eclecticism — for they said he was as spellbinding as a whole troupe of musicians — and the ornamental nature of his fine body.

"Of course, his music is false, according to nature," said the dour troubadour to his wife, thinking of its plagiarist origins, "but it is beautiful, that I will say for him." This as he watched his long-lost *chansonnier* being fished out of the Seine.

The woman said to the man as they leant over the parapet, "You can have it, for what it's worth, but it will always be mine."

The man's eyes filled with tears. He wanted to turn and walk along the promenade, past Notre Dame, out of sight, but just at that moment he could not bring himself to.

(Dragging the river: after the *Oxford Companion*)

By the end of the Sixteenth Century, *musica ficta* was so integrated into the tonal system that it no longer went under that name, but was seen as the norm.

(Divinity: after himself)

For two pins I will tell you a divine dream.
Oh my collapsible sleep!
I once met a soffit, her name
soft to the touch, I put out my hand,
touched her. She was soft but
inaccessible, this combination alluring.
My breath filled the chamber of a sackbut
red as an opium den, heavy
and sweet, and from that place

which sounds like the heart, beats like it,
flew into the sky.
Beloved!
Moments I have heard the chance music
of the divine plan of God.
Oh my dusty ornament!
How I dusted you!
I could see everything perfectly
the unseen — of you I saw nothing.
How I wanted the sound of your voice!
It's not a question of who notated
everything, or who invented, made up
after a quarrel, but who loved.
I loved you but you were
impossible!
A suite of stories to explain . . .
It is not necessary to explain.
. . . Why I have lost love, it has dribbled
through the anxious lattice of my fingers.
You! Beloved! Little Saint!
Love! You can explain if you like
but a story will never change anything.
I know.
A contentment made of real things
I will stray from occasionally
perhaps oftener on your account.
When the dream went, love went
— where? Can it be destroyed?
Doesn't it travel on forever
looking for Heaven?
Transferred like soundwaves to another medium,
wood, or the divine flooding of veins.
You were always good at physics.
I no longer hear you. Your body
I touched often, you have removed your
body, which is the intention of the soul.
The Ficta *is where you have touched me*
— am I the author because I did not love enough?
This is the love, its body.

I am
the author but I have surrendered everything.

I set out to write what I knew but instead I have written what I wondered, and a man is the author of these astonishments.